Gaillac trained the gun on the frightened man. The entire cabaret grew silent.

"Do you know who I am?" Gaillac asked.

"Yes, Monsieur Gaillac," the bartender replied in a hoarse whisper.

"And yet you see fit to ridicule me?"

"It w-was an accident, monsieur," the old man said, stammering. "These old legs of mine, they do not work as well as they used to."

"And now," Gaillac said, "they will not work at all."

He made a move to squeeze the trigger, thought better of it, and turned to Kinski.

"Here, Petrovich," he said, tossing the gun to Kinski. "You take care of him. Any man working for me kills my enemies."

THE MARAUDERS

CAPTAIN "CRAZY JACK" KEENAN—The ultimate warrior. He doesn't need a weapon, he is a weapon.

SERGEANT CHAN—A deadly marksman who never misses.

CPO FREDDIE MAMUDI—A knife-wielding Afghan freedom fighter.

LIEUTENANT KINSKI—A human death machine who rocks-and-rolls with an assault rifle instead of a guitar.

THE MARAUDERS
LIAR'S DICE

Michael McGann

J

JOVE BOOKS, NEW YORK

THE MARAUDERS: LIAR'S DICE

A Jove Book/published by arrangement with
the author

PRINTING HISTORY
Jove edition/February 1990

ISBN: 0-515-10284-9

Jove Books are published by The Berkley Publishing Group,
200 Madison Avenue, New York, New York 10016.
The name "JOVE" and the "J" logo
are trademarks belonging to Jove Publications, Inc.

PRINTED IN THE UNITED STATES OF AMERICA

10   9   8   7   6   5   4   3   2   1

For
John William Corrington (1932–1988),
The Old Man Among His Flowers

ONE

Jean Gaillac didn't like to consider himself French. He was a citizen of the world. Yeah, he thought to himself, that's what he was. What did he need any country for? What did he care about the government? He got by. That's what counted.

Gaillac guided his jeep down the country road, toward the village of Bliers in Southern France. He wasn't too far from Montpellier. Maybe, after he was finished, he'd take the car and head for the city. Get a little liquored. Get a little crazy. Spill a little blood.

He smiled to himself. He could get away with it too. He was an official.

He nearly laughed out loud. Now that was a joke.

He glanced at the truckful of men riding behind him. Local yokels, mostly. Country boys recruited because of their abundance of strength and lack of brains. Still, they took orders. That's all that counted with Jean.

Jean had been in Paris when World War III broke out. He didn't remember how old he was then. Didn't really know his age now, for that matter. Maybe he was thirty. Time didn't matter anymore. In the survival game, nothing mattered but keeping a foothold. Making sure you didn't slip down a notch.

His mother had been Vietnamese, one of the refugees who had headed for France in the late sixties. His father had been French. Both had died during the food riots following the nuke-out. Stupid, that. They had owned a restaurant. Vietnamese.

Both had decided to defend it against looters.

Bad move.

The stupid thing was that if the rioters had seen what in-

1

gredients had gone into the food, they would have turned tail and run to Italy. At least they had pasta there. It's hard to screw up pasta.

After the rioting died down, Jean decided to leave Paris. He found out, very quickly, that his tall, bulky body allowed him to bully most people who tried to slow him down. It was only a matter of time before he killed someone.

And before long he had.

With his bare hands. Since that time, of course, he had become quite a master of the blade and the gun. In fact, he could handle about any weapon now.

He didn't take pride in that, it was just something he had found necessary to learn. People would kill you if you didn't kill them first.

He had been making out okay when the FSE troops moved into France. The French rolled over and just let them in. If it hadn't been so pathetic, it would have been funny. The Federated States of Europe represented itself as a unifying force, a really tightly knit government, bringing all the countries of Europe together in one harmonious blob.

But Jean had known better from the outset. As a thug himself, he could spot other thugs, no matter how pretty their uniforms. When big, bearded FSE Chairman General Yevgeny Maximov and his stooge, Igor Vesensky, started sweet-talking the populace with promises of plenty and warning about the dastardly forces of the United States, Jean figured that he'd better join the FSE and soon.

The French didn't have a chance against these snake-oil salesmen. Kiss up to them, scratch them on the back of the ear, and they'd wag their national tail appreciatively, like some half-starved street mutt.

For a year or two the FSE bled the people and the land dry. The people, for the most part, didn't understand what was going on. No matter how hard they worked, they never seemed to get ahead.

Jean had understood, though. He had seen it happen time and time again in the streets of Paris. The ones at the top stayed there by keeping the ones at the bottom firmly in place.

And so, with constant reassurances from the FSE, the people of France—indeed, the people of Europe—continued to toil. The FSE continued to smile and to take.

Then, a year ago, things started getting squirrelly. The British Isles ran the FSE troops out of their kingdom. Rumors spread throughout Europe that they had been assisted by a crack band of American commandos, the Marauders. Some said the band consisted of four, some said four hundred.

It didn't matter much to Jean, but it had mattered a lot to the FSE. They stopped talking to the citizens of Europe and began acting.

Which is how Jean became an official FSE representative. It wasn't a bad deal—transportation, all the weaponry you needed, regular pay plus whatever fringe benefits he could imagine.

Maximov and his French stooge, Giles Robespierre, got wind of an underground army—Free France—and pretty much lost their cool. Martial law was declared. French citizens were no longer permitted to own private handguns, even those who lived deep in the countryside and relied on hunting to put food on their tables.

And the Goon Squads were created.

Actually, they were called the Federated Guards, but it was pretty obvious exactly what they were, official title or no: packs of men, eager for a little money and a lot of power who roamed the countryside, "encouraging" small communities to cooperate fully with the new FSE mandates and to turn over any and all countrymen they knew to be part of the traitorous Free France movement.

Some cooperated, some didn't. Those that didn't . . . well, that was how Jean made his living.

Gaillac's jeep zoomed past the first farmhouse of the small town of Bliers. Robespierre wanted the town taught a lesson. It seemed that the farmers of the area weren't handing over enough of their crops into the national till. The hoarding of food wasn't encouraged these days, especially since it might be intended to feed an underground army.

Jean guided his auto into the small town square. The village's lone Catholic church, bell hanging high atop a steeple, stood at the end of the square.

Jean allowed the jeep to slow to a stop. Switching off the ignition, he climbed out of the auto and walked over to the church. He glanced around. A few villagers peeked out of their homes from parted curtains. No one emerged from any of the buildings.

Jean sighed. This was getting to be a tiresome routine. He turned toward his "troops" in the truck.

"Four of you, take the truck out to the farmlands. Bring back anybody you find. The rest of you, take your places on the road. No one is to enter or leave this village."

Ten gawky young men skittered out of the flatbed and jogged to the outskirts of town. The remaining four sent the truck rumbling out toward the countryside.

Jean watched his "troops" waddle into position.

Morons, he thought. They would have been easy prey for any Parisian thug, even the novices.

Jean swung an AK-47 from over his shoulder and aimed it at the bell tower.

He squeezed off a torrent of rounds. The shells hammered into the old bell, eventually shredding it, but not before forcing the bell to emit the strangest come-to-meeting clanging it had ever attempted in its community-service career.

As the last shards of the timeworn bell tumbled down onto the street, Jean Gaillac tilted his head back and bellowed, "People of Bliers! I am Gaillac of the FSE. You are to come out of your homes and businesses and assemble in the town square—now. Repeat: You are to assemble in the town square immediately. Those who refuse to obey this order will be punished. You have three minutes. Then we shall start house-to-house searches."

Jean glanced around at the town. The village couldn't have been supplying the government with that much food. The FSE must really fear the underground, Gaillac concluded.

Doors began to open all around him.

One by one the villagers of Bliers shambled out of their homes and stores.

They were old people for the most part. Most of the strong, young ones, Jean reasoned, would be out in the fields. A small schoolhouse at the far end of the village disgourged two dozen or so children, all under the age of sixteen.

Jean glanced at the gaggle of kids heading his way, accompanied by a nun who seemed to be mummified. A couple of the young girls looked good. Really good.

Jean raised his rifle and pointed to a spot in front of the

church. The townspeople gathered. Jean signaled for two of his men to start a house-to-house search.

The fourth house checked produced an elderly man, wearing a beret and a bulky sweater. The man fought and kicked the FSE man as he was dragged out into the street.

Silly bastard, Jean thought with a sigh. He probably still thought he was fighting World War II.

Jean nodded at his man. The young hayseed tossed the old man onto the ground, pulled out an old Luger, and, as the crowd gasped, blew the top of his head off.

Jean turned to the crowd. "I am not playing a game" was all he said.

Just then the truck pulled back into town, twenty young men and eight older ones jammed into the back like cattle. The truck rolled into the town square. The four FSE men on board motioned with their rifles, directing the men into the town square.

The searching of the homes stopped.

Jean turned to the villagers of Bliers. "My fellow citizens," he said, growing weary of the speech the more he gave it, "I have been sent here by your government, the Federated States of Europe, and its representative, Giles Robespierre, to investigate a food shortage."

The people glanced at each other nervously. "As you all know, by law you are required to contribute half of your yearly crops to the National Food Foundation. Your yield this past growing season, according to our records, shows a thirty-percent drop."

Jean felt the need to pace back and forth before the people but fought it. *Stand tall*, he thought, *make them look at your face.* So he shook his head from side to side instead, allowing his shaggy brown locks to tumble down onto his forehead. "The weather this past season should have provided a larger than normal yield. So if the weather was in favor of your growing season, where did the food go, eh?"

"The ground," one old man said. "The ground is poison. The crops, they shrivel. We do the best we can."

Jean smiled, exposing two dimples and two rows of crooked teeth. "Interesting."

The old man nodded. "Terrible."

"Perhaps these *shriveled* crops . . . you hide them? Perhaps you give them to your friends? Friends the FSE knows about and are hunting down like dogs?"

The crowd murmured in dissent. "That is not so!" an old woman declared. "We know nothing of Free France."

"But you've heard of them, eh?"

"Of course," the old woman replied. "Who has not?"

"And you know about their American friends?"

"Yes," the old woman said, cackling. "The army of freedom fighters!"

"They are traitors to our cause," Jean announced.

"We have no cause," the old man called out. "We are farmers."

"Correction," Jean said. "You *were* farmers."

Jean thought hard. He couldn't prove the villagers were aiding the resistance, but he didn't like their attitude. A little too cocky, especially the older ones. If he left them alone, he'd be reprimanded by his superiors and someone else would be sent to Bliers. He stared at the frightened, yet defiant, faces of the villagers.

Oh, screw it.

He had no kinship with them.

He was Jean Gaillac, citizen of the world. He had no homeland. He had no family. He owed allegiance to no one.

He motioned for his "troops" to move in. The crowd was segregated into groups.

Men over the age of sixteen were forced into one corner of the town square. The old people were useless to the FSE. The younger, stronger ones were a threat. If they were old enough to work the fields, they were old enough to learn how to fight back.

Another group consisted of women over forty. Useless, except for fun. Getting too old to bear children, too fat to work hard, too passive to assault.

A third group was the remainder of the women, from the children to those in their late thirties. Breeding material. Young bodies that could be molded into *any* type of function, from tilling the fields to working the FSE-owned and -operated clubs in Marseilles and the other big cities.

The last group consisted of boys—young pups, mostly, too young to become guerrillas but old enough to work hard for the FSE.

Jean made sure each of the groups stood far apart from the other. He motioned to his troops.

The hayseed goons walked up to the first group of men and, without warning, opened fire with M16s. The goons were not exactly marksmen, but the arcing motion of the gun barrels did the trick. Jean smiled as the bodies began to whirl and twirl, like broken marionettes. Several of the younger men raised their hands before their faces in a vain attempt to avoid the lethal sting of the slugs.

Women wailed and children cried as the blazing rifle muzzles swept over the first group again and again.

It interested Jean, this carnage. The young ones, the virile ones, were almost always the first to bolt and run, to plead and beg. But the old men? They stood there and took it. Stood leaning on their canes, squinting at the enemy for as long as they could. Some died with clenched fists. Jean realized that their posing wasn't the result of mere pain. These old dinosaurs were the biggest threat to the FSE. Many of them had taken on Hitler. Many of them would again, if they had the chance.

Jean chuckled. If it wasn't so ineffective a gesture, he could almost consider it noble.

But, he reminded himself, farmers were idiots. They knew nothing of nobility. Wheat, barley, hog slop—that was their vile little universe.

Within a minute the first group of villagers was nothing more than a mound of bleeding, pulverized flesh.

Several of the younger women in the third group tried to run to their martyred husbands and fathers.

Jean calmly turned his AK-47 on them, raking the ground before their feet. Plumes of dust spat up at the women's faces. They stopped their charge. Sobbing, they returned to their herd.

"Good girls." Jean smiled.

Jean's goons marched over to the second group, the older women.

"Good-bye, ladies," Jean said, nodding to his men.

Again the air was filled with the monstrous roar of angry guns.

The older women shrieked as the automatic fire sliced into their soft, white skin. Jean watched in fascination as the old nun was hit over and over by burning lead. He was amazed that such an old, frail body contained that much blood.

When the shooting stopped, three quarters of the village's population lay bleeding on the street.

Jean turned to the other two groups. "I do not play games, people," he announced. "The FSE does not play games. You want to raise heroes? There are your heroes."

He pointed to the two flesh-colored mounds of refuse in the street. "There is a lesson to be learned here. The FSE is good to its citizens when the citizens are good to the FSE. Defy the FSE and you will die. This is simple, no? You cannot fight off guns with bread and butter and pitchforks."

He walked toward his jeep, calling over his shoulder. "François? Radio Robespierre. Tell him we have a shipment for his dens in Marseilles. You and the rest will remain here with the villagers until the new mayor arrives."

"What shall we do with them until the mayor arrives?" the youth named François asked.

"Whatever you want to. Enjoy yourselves. You have women, girls, boys. Let your imagination be your guide. Oh, yes. Be careful during your play period. Leave most of these people intact afterward. The new mayor will want workers for his fields, workers who will produce crops for the National Food Foundation."

"And the bodies?"

"You can burn them," Jean said. "If that's too troublesome, when you're done with your fun time, let the ladies and fellows bury their dead. Just don't leave the bodies on the streets too long. We don't need the stench or the disease, okay?"

"Where will *you* be, sir?"

"Anywhere."

Jean caught sight of a wide-eyed brunette in the crowd of young women. A schoolgirl, still dressed in her oversize blouse and drab, faded plaid skirt. He pointed to her. "You. Come here, please."

The girl swallowed hard and, leaving her group, walked slowly toward the jeep.

Jean watched the quivering figure approach him. "And what is your name?"

"Lucille," the little girl replied.

"That is a nice name."

"Thank you, sir."

"Would you like to come for a ride with me, Lucille?"

"I . . . I don't think so."

Jean smiled at the child. "How old are you, Lucille?"

"Twelve."

"Old enough." Jean smiled, thrusting his hand down her blouse and locating her stiff bra immediately. "Now get in the jeep, girl."

The girl began to cry. Jean liked that. He liked that a lot. He hoisted the screaming girl into the jeep and sent the engine roaring to life.

He headed for the deep countryside.

Lucille was wailing now.

Jean laughed out loud, pulling the child closer to him. Soon she'd stop wailing.

Soon she'd get to know Jean Gaillac.

Her first and last lover.

After that the birds could have her.

TWO

The city of London was quiet as Big Ben chimed midnight. Eleven-o'clock curfews were still in effect, and stores and homes were still required to mask all lights after sundown. There were no evening showings of old movies in the decaying movie theaters. The West End boasted no plays. The atmosphere was as oppressive as the night fog was thick.

Still, the English, the Irish, and the Scots had managed to wrestle the strangling grip of the Federated States of Europe from all their territories and were more determined than ever to keep them out.

They knew it meant sacrifice, but they didn't seem to mind.

All of the United Kingdom was truly united now, under the watchful eye of a new king, Willis "Shatterhand" MacGregor, a former Scottish cop who had had his right hand mangled by FSE goons in an effort to ensure cooperation. The effort had backfired. The big, bearded, fiery-haired man had only to look at the studded leather glove on his right hand for a source of revolutionary inspiration.

He decided to gather the clans of Scotland and fight back . . . in a surprisingly major way.

Backing him up had been five misfit American guerrillas: the Marauders. There were four now, but they were the grandest fighters small-town cop MacGregor had ever seen. They were also probably his best friends in this post-nuked-out hell of a world.

That was why MacGregor sat stewing in his office at the palace.

He was about to send them out on a suicide mission.

Again.

He heard the door to his office ease open. "Come in, fellows," he muttered, staring at the maps and typed reports on his desk.

Captain John F. "Crazy Jack" Keenan, former Green Beret and present gonzo giant, strode into the room. "You're not much on security, your Kingliness." He grinned, rubbing a callused paw through his tangle of red hair.

He eased himself into a chair. "I could have been an assassin."

"In that case you would have been shot down on the stairway, Jack," Shatterhand said, not looking up. "There are men behind the tapestries."

"And I thought they were just big moths," Jack said, in mock incredulity.

"Where are the others?"

"They'll be along presently. Buddha, Chan, Freddie, and Kinski had some late homework with your troops. I came here to chat."

"And stall?"

"That too. How goes the battle for hearts and minds?"

Shatterhand smiled and leaned back in his chair, rubbing his mangled, gloved hand. "Could be better. Could be worse. Prime Minister Spivvy is doing a good job. Elections for Parliament are scheduled. Unemployment is down. People are getting by."

"I sense a *but* coming." Jack smiled.

"Three butts present and accounted for." Lieutenant Peter Kinski said, strolling into the room. "You get paid extra for overtime?"

"Afraid not," Shatterhand said.

"Well, you should," Gunnery Sergeant Winston S. "Buddha" Chan said, waddling into the room. "Your tapestries need their boots shined."

CPO Farouz "Freddie" Mamudi slunk into the room and slithered down into a couch. "They need to change their cologne too."

Shatterhand stared at the four men: his staunchest allies. Buddha was of English and Mongol descent and had been USMC-trained. Bald, golden-sunglasses-encased, he had been the best sniper in the Marine Corps and quite a master of martial arts.

Mamudi was a former Navy SEAL and all-around ladies' man. The slender Sunni Muslim was handsome, but for a long scar he called his "zipper," which ran along his hairline and across his right eye, of glass. Both imperfections gifts of a Soviet sniper in Afghanistan. What Shatterhand loved most about Mamudi was his penchant for selecting a different glass eye for different occasions. Tonight he was displaying an orb with a small lion's head in its iris.

Kinski was an Air Force vet of Polish ancestry. He could fly anything that remotely hinted at having wings, jerry-build anything that ran on electricity, and lie like the devil himself. When not fighting, the tall, thin man cared greatly for his blond Fabian-like pompadour haircut, something he seemed to laminate each day.

And then there was Crazy Jack. What could Shatterhand say about Crazy Jack? He lived up to his name, that was for sure. A funny, surly, cantankerous mountain of a man, Jack hated authority, inaction, and politics. He did, however, love carousing. Since arriving in the U.K., Crazy Jack had run up a bar tab of nearly $10,000, most of it for damages. Jack made a game out of being gruff. It was a good way to hide his well-above-average IQ. The man had a combined M.S. in chemistry and physics and actually wrote a few books on New Age physics before the big nuke-out.

"You were talking about butts?" Kinski reminded King Shatterhand while running a comb through his golden waves of hair. "Pretty ones?"

"No." Shatterhand sighed. "Pretty damned ugly, in fact."

"Then, fuggem," Kinski sighed. "Where there's an ugly butt, there's an ugly face to go with it."

"Kinski," Crazy Jack growled.

Kinski slid a little lower in his chair. "Just a little humor."

"What's up, MacGregor?"

"Well, as you all know," Shatterhand began, "our armed forces are slowly getting back into working order—thanks, mostly, to you boys. You've all been excellent teachers, craftsmen, scavengers. Enlistment in the military is up enormously. For the first time since World War II, there is a spirit of patriotism here. Our young lads want to stand up to the FSE."

"They're not ready," Buddha Chan said, removing his golden shooter's glasses and polishing them slowly. "Not by a long shot."

"That's true," Kinski pointed out. "We'd need a shaykh, pir—a mystical guide—to pull our troops through a confrontation at this point."

"And we've lost our guide," Buddha Chan said, referring to Tom Bee, the oldest of the original Marauders, an American Indian who proved to be totally in sync with the forces of nature.

"In six months *maybe* they'll be combat-ready," Crazy Jack injected.

"I know, I know," Shatterhand said, running his left hand through his beard. "But conditions in Europe are worsening. We have some informants in what was once Interpol, and FSE violence is on the rise throughout western Europe. For some reason the former Commonwealth countries are being singled out."

"Maybe it's because they're not used to dictators," Kinski said with a thin smile.

"Those FSE bastards," Jack said. "They've really tightened the screws since Ireland tossed them out."

"Yeah." Kinski nodded. "Some people have no sense of humor."

"There are mass executions," Shatterhand said. "Public torture. Small farmers are being 'disappeared,' their land being taken over by FSE-appointed 'mayors,' and their families forced to work it."

"Sounds like serfdom," Buddha said.

"Sounds like Nazism to me," Mamudi muttered.

"It sounds like *shit*," Crazy Jack whispered, simmering. "So what you're saying is that because of our efforts, the people of Europe are getting the shit kicked out of them, and we don't have the manpower to back them up."

"That's about the size of it," Shatterhand said.

"But what about the resistance groups?" Mamudi asked. "There are rumors that all over Europe underground armies are rising up."

"Not quite rising," Shatterhand said. "With the new FSE

mandates in effect, it's very difficult for them to get hold of firepower. Most of them hid their weapons when the mandates were issued, but they're still badly undermanned and outnumbered. Plus, there's the problem of leadership.

"We know the most about Free France. It's a solid outfit and growing. But in the past six months, half of their leaders, mostly farm people, have been executed. We have a direct link with them. They've begged us for help. I—I'm sorry, boys, but I couldn't refuse."

Kinski swallowed hard. "Why are you apologizing?"

"Because . . ."

"Because we're the only help you can spare," Jack said, chuckling. "Oh, I love this. When do we leave?"

"Now wait a minute," Kinski said. "What about tactics? Military strategy? Backup?"

"When have we ever worried about that?" Buddha said, scratching his round, bald head.

"We are four warriors"—Mamudi grinned—"in the tradition of the great Suleiman."

"Never met him," Kinski said. "Never want to. Look, MacGregor, we can't *always* be a four-man invasion force. It doesn't make sense."

"Neither does senseless slaughter, does it?" Shatterhand pointed out.

"Well, no," Kinski said, already feeling foolish. "Of course not."

"And the fact that you may save countless lives by just being there, just to give the French people someone to rally around? That doesn't seem important to you?"

"Well, of course it does." Kinski gulped. The other three Marauders were grinning at him. "Oh, the hell with it. Tell our president we're all in agreement."

"Already have," Shatterhand said. "Radioed him this afternoon."

"Pretty sure of yourself, aren't you, Your Highness?" Jack said, crossing his massive arms across his barrel chest.

"No," Shatterhand replied with a wink. "I'm sure of *you*."

Kinski muttered something in Polish. It had something to do with where to place a kielbasa and did not contain the phrase *Have a nice day*.

"Now," Shatterhand said, "gather 'round, lads. And I'll show you the plan."

"This should be good," Kinski said.

"Our radio contact is a woman named Marie Marrette. She's been with the Free France movement since its inception. It started out as a few villagers in the Northern part of the country who were tired of being victimized by both the roving postwar scavenger gangs *and* the FSE troops. They started shooting at both. The ones who weren't executed went underground. They have quite a neat little network set up throughout the country. We're not sure of their numbers, but we're sure of their zeal.

"Marie will be your contact. Right now we're planning for you to go in and run a few guerrilla strikes. Something very public and very embarrassing to the FSE."

"How long are we in-country for?" Jack asked.

"For as long as it takes to destablize the FSE," Shatterhand said.

"Give us a week," Buddha said, laughing. "We'll have them diving off the Eiffel Tower."

"How far can we take it?" Freddie asked.

"As far as you have to. Avoid any injuries to civilians, of course. We want to make converts as well as gear up Free France. The worse the FSE looks in their eyes, the better our chances of galvanizing the population. If you have to cut and run a few times to save your butts and those of innocent civilians, do so. I need you there alive and percolating. I don't want any grand last stands."

Mamudi nodded. "'Winning one hundred battles in one hundred outings is not the highest skill; rather, it is being able to force the enemy to surrender; that is the ultimate,'" he said, quoting Sun Tzu.

"God bless you," Kinski said with a smirk.

"Where's the drop zone?" Jack asked innocently.

"I'm afraid the only place we could come up with that was convenient, both geographically and in terms of Free France's nearest enclave, was a place that has been used before."

He placed his finger firmly on a place located on the northwest coast of France.

"Holy jeezus," Jack whispered. "The beaches of Normandy?"

"We have a small skiff awaiting your arrival at Brighton. You'll be armed, of course, but not excessively so. You'll be going in under the cover of darkness to Le Havre. Once you're in the water, the skiff will return to Brighton and file a complete report to me. Members of Free France will rendezvous with you on the beach, supplying you with additional weaponry and providing an escort to one of their outposts."

"When do we leave?" Jack asked.

"As soon as possible," Shatterhand replied.

"Is tomorrow too soon?" Mamudi asked.

"Tomorrow would be perfect." Shatterhand nodded.

"Good." Freddie grinned. "That gives me time to polish my cat's-eye."

THREE

Giles Robespierre did not fit in with life in Paris, even during the FSE occupation. A small, rodentlike man with bushy eyebrows and a shock of white hair, the well-dressed stooge was more comfortable in his hometown of Marseilles. He had made a good living there for years, smuggling guns, drugs, and whatever was illegal at the time to eager buyers via an intricate network of black marketeers.

It was Robespierre's constant contact with the underground that had first brought him to the attention of the FSE. He had a police record that, when stacked from the floor, was actually taller than Giles; yet he never served any appreciable jail time and, more often than not, got off on a technicality.

This impressed the FSE greatly. They needed a weasel to oversee France. And in their eyes, Robespierre was the biggest weasel around.

The tiny man paced back and forth in his hotel suite near the Champs-Elysées. Two FSE men in the next room were in the process of "chatting" with a prisoner, purported to be part of the ephemeral Free France resistance.

A man named Lyonnes.

Robespierre began to hum to himself as the screams from the next room grew louder.

He spun around as the door to his room swung open. The clouded expression on Robespierre's face evaporated immediately.

"Jean!" he exclaimed. "It is so good to see you!"

Jean Gaillac sauntered into the room, glancing at the ornate furnishings. "Nice flat, Giles," he said, slamming his burly body down onto a plush couch.

Giles pulled out a French cigarette and lit it, filling the room with a smell resembling burning rubber. "You're a little far from home, aren't you, Giles?"

"Orders." Giles shrugged. "The chairman wanted me to come up here and talk to you personally."

Jean frowned. "Is there some sort of problem with my work?"

"Oh, no, no," Giles said, skittering over to the big man. "Just the opposite. Your work has been conspicuously excellent. Very good. Very good, indeed."

"So what's the problem? I haven't been in Paris since I was a kid."

"I realize that, but it is a good headquarters for our next assignment."

"Our?"

"Yes, I have been asked to supervise you in a very special operation."

The man in the next room screamed.

Jean didn't bother to flinch. He had heard worse. "Practicing dentistry next door?"

"A country boy," Giles replied. "We think he knows something about Free France. I have a network of informants, you see, and—"

"So you caught yourself a Free Frenchie." Jean shrugged. "What's the big deal?"

"We believe an invasion force is on its way to our shores," Robespierre blurted.

"How big?"

"We don't know."

"Where's the landing site?"

"We don't know that, either."

"Well, you don't know one hell of a lot, do you, Giles?" Jean said, struggling out of the deep-cushioned couch. "Want me to find out a few things for you?"

"If you please." Giles nodded.

"Get your assholes out of there," Jean said with a sigh.

Giles trotted over to the door and knocked on it. "Men, stop the interrogation."

Two FSE men in full uniform marched out of the room, their square, Eastern European jaws glimmering with sweat.

Jean smirked. Fuggin' Russian boys. Cared too much about appearance and too little about results.

Giles made a move to introduce the soldiers to Jean. Jean waved him off. "Later. What's the guy's name in there?"

"Edouard Lyonnes."

"You need a lot of information or just a little?"

"Not too much. Details on the invasion."

"Good," Jean said. "Get either a body bag or some sheets up here."

Giles nodded, motioning for the two soldiers to bring what Jean needed.

Jean walked into the bedroom. A young black-haired man with wild brown eyes sat sagging in a wooden chair. His arms and legs were bound. His face was a mass of bruises. His eyes were swollen nearly shut.

He gazed up at Jean. Jean eased the door closed behind him. "So, Edouard," Giles said, smiling, "these Russians haven't been treating you so good, eh?"

Edouard shook his head from side to side. "I have nothing to say, monsieur."

"With the way your lips are swollen, I'd say that's an understatement."

Jean pulled a chair up in front of the young man. "But they were Russian. I am French, no?"

"You work for the FSE?"

"Now and then."

"Then you are not French."

"Yeah, yeah, yeah." Jean sighed. "And here's the part where you spit on my shoes or something, except you probably don't have the saliva for it."

The boy twisted his swollen lips into what passed for a smirk. "In my mind, however, I can picture it."

"Okay, Edouard, let's cut the crap. I can hum 'The Marseillaise' and march around the room if it'll make you feel more of a patriot, but you've gotten yourself into some very deep shit here.

"That little fellow outside? Monsieur Mouse? He's very big within the FSE. He thinks you're aiding and abetting Free France."

"I have nothing to say."

"No?"

"Until my dying breath."

"Well, my young, freedom-fighting farm boy, that's probably going to come soon. Once I leave, those two Ruskies are going to come in and do the cancan on your skull. Have you ever seen a man beaten to death?"

"Of course not."

Jean nodded. "No, of course not. Few people have. It's a very slow process. Bones tend to splinter and crack. Flesh splits. One eye can be knocked out. Your nose broken. Jaw snapped. Ribs smashed. Fingers mangled one by one. It's a pretty painful experience, let me tell you."

"Then I will be a martyr for my cause."

Jean whistled through his teeth. "You *are* young, aren't you? Look, friend, I don't know how to break this to you, but nobody is going to know that you died for your cause. For all they know, you took a vacation in Paris, hooked up with a showgirl, and moved to the north country. Do you think those Russians will allow anybody to see your body? You're either going to wind up as maggot munchies or fish food at the bottom of the Seine. You will just vanish from the face of the earth as far as your friends and family are concerned."

"You do not frighten me, monsieur."

Jean nodded. "Well, then, you're pretty naïve."

"You may leave me now," the battered young man said with a sneer.

"Not until I get what I came for."

"And what is that?"

"Information on an invasion force."

"I know nothing about it."

"Who's behind it? The Brits?"

"As I said—"

"Are the Marauders involved?"

"I know nothing."

"Where are they landing?"

Edouard stared at him defiantly. "How many times must I repeat myself?"

Jean sighed. He produced a serrated knife and held it before the beaten man's eyes. "This is getting tiresome, Edouard. I'm trying to save you a beating here. Show a little class, eh?"

"You are no better than the rest of them. I can see it in your eyes."

"You're wrong there, my young friend. I'm *worse*. Here, I'll show you."

Edouard gulped as Jean lowered the knife to his midsection. Jean smiled and moved the knife toward one of the young man's bound and bleeding hands. Jean slashed the ropes holding down the man's left hand.

He slowly lifted Edouard's hand. "Ah, this must hurt you quite a bit, no, the circulation being cut off for so long?"

Edouard winced as his numb arm suddenly came alive with tiny pinpricks of pain.

"Now, as I mentioned before," Jean continued, "I came in here for information. I will not leave until I get it."

"There is nothing you can do to me," Edouard declared; rather foolishly, Jean thought.

Jean pulled out a 9-mm pistol and placed the muzzle flat into the palm of Edouard's outstretched hand. The young man's eyes widened from beneath their puffy edges.

"Think, again, Edouard," Jean said, squeezing the trigger.

The young man's hand blew apart in several pieces, sending a thick fount of blood, flesh, and bone sailing into the bedroom wall behind him. It hit with a splat as Edouard let out a deafening shriek of pain.

Jean allowed the arm to drop. Blood gushed from the young man's pulpy wrist.

"Now," Jean declared, "you can either tell me the information or I can let you bleed to death . . . after I remove your other hand and, perhaps, if I get really enthusiastic, your feet as well. Tell me what I want and I will get you medical attention."

The young man's mouth began to quiver. His head rolled back and forth. He began whispering. Jean leaned closer, nodding thoughtfully as the boy squeezed out word after word.

When Edouard had stopped talking, Jean straightened and smiled.

"Thank you, Edouard. You have earned peace, eh?"

Jean pressed the muzzle of the gun just below the frightened young man's left temple. He discharged a round, sending the boy's brains tumbling onto the floor.

The force of the impact sent Edouard and the chair tipping back onto the floor. Jean watched with moderate interest as the boy's nervous system kicked in, sending his lifeless legs and torso twitching.

Jean wondered from how many chickens Edouard had coaxed a similar performance on his farm.

"They don't make patriots like they used to, eh?" Jean muttered, walking out of the room.

Giles Robespierre stood, quivering with rage, in the next room as Jean entered.

"You killed him!" Robespierre nearly squealed.

"You're pretty observant, Giles," Jean said, walking over to a wet bar and pouring himself three fingers of Scotch. He downed it without ice.

"But you were only in there for a few minutes! My men were in there for over an hour."

"And didn't get a single piece of information out of him," Jean said, refilling his glass. "Got a pencil and a piece of paper?"

"Yes . . ."

"Well, grab them and use them, Giles," Jean said, staring at the rodentlike man. How the hell did this man become a mobster in Marseilles? He seemed afraid of his own shadow.

He watched Giles prepare to take notes. "The invasion force is landing at Le Havre tonight at 2400 hours."

Giles glanced at him strangely.

"Midnight, Giles," Jean continued. "They'll be arriving in rafts, so there shouldn't be too many of them. It's a combined effort of your Free France friends and the Brits. The actual invasion force will be spearheaded by your Yankee heroes."

"The Marauders?"

"The same," Jean said. "Want me to be there to meet them?"

"But of course! What do you need?"

"Two dozen men, and I mean *good* men, not the farm boys I'm working with in the Goon Squad. Can you get me professional soldiers?"

"Certainly, we have many trained men in the Paris area. It is, after all, one of our largest cities. The third largest port in all of France, next to Le Havre and Marseilles, of course."

"I took history, Giles. These men. Can any of them speak French?"

"Well, no . . ."

"How about English? I can get by in English."

"Yes. Definitely. Chairman Maximov prides himself on how well his Eastern bloc men can communicate."

"Good for him."

"They might not have proper uniforms, however. Many of them have been working underground, which is, in fact, how I got my information on—"

"I don't care about the uniforms. I need men who can handle weapons."

"They are experts, I assure you."

Jean heaved a heavy sigh. Talking to Giles was like communicating with a bowl of day-old soup. "I'll need a few machine guns, rocket launchers, and two flatbed trucks."

"It's done."

"Good. Now, is there a place in this museum I can nap in for a few hours?"

"Certainly, certainly. I will arrange a room for you at once."

"How long will that take?"

"Less than an hour."

"Too long."

"I will put my best men on it."

The weasel known as Giles put a wiry arm around the shambling giant. "We will teach those vermin a lesson tonight, eh, Jean? We will show those Americans and those British scum just how powerful we are. How powerful the FSE is!"

"*We'll* teach them a lesson?" Jean said, gazing down at Robespierre from beneath his heavy eyelids. "Have you decided to come with us, then?"

"Well, no," Robespierre said. "I have, uh, many duties here. Things to coordinate, et cetera."

"Right," Jean said, walking out of the room and into a hallway. "Then I guess *I'll* teach them a lesson and *you'll* report it to the FSE. Maybe they'll give you a few more cookies, eh?"

The shaggy-haired Parisian lumbered down the hall, leaving a startled Robespierre in his wake.

Jean Gaillac stopped in front of a hotel room. He pounded

on the door with his ham-sized fists. "Inside! Hey!"

A fat older man appeared at the door. "What is it you want?"

"I want to sleep."

"But this is *my* room!" the porcine Parisian replied.

Jean grabbed the man by the throat and swung him around, sending him smashing into the opposite wall. "It *was* your room," Jean said, stalking into the empty flat and slamming the door closed behind him.

FOUR

Under the dark shroud of a starless night, the small skiff sputtered across the wave-tossed English Channel, a tall, grizzled man named Bidoff at the helm.

The four Marauders readied themselves below. Buddha Chan spent his time either scratching his bald head impatiently or checking his war-scarred scoped M14 for the umpteenth time.

Mamudi, sure that they were heading into a hand-to-hand combat zone, made sure his fighting knives were securely fashioned to his utility belt: the V-42 stiletto; the Steele/Randel fighting knife; the Al Mar/Uzan Oda SHIVA; his double-horn Poignards; double-short "Gim"; and his two butterfly knives.

Kinski stared with apprehension at the water swirling in the boat's wake, ignoring his Armalite 180, his treasured AK-47, and a Remington 870 pump-action 12-gauge riot shotgun.

"I have a bad feeling about this, Jack," he said to Keenan.

"Don't worry about it," Jack said, feeling slightly queasy from the constant rocking of the boat. "We've been in worse situations."

"But those were on land," Kinski said.

"I have my junior lifesaving badge on me somewhere," Jack replied, "and Freddie was a SEAL. You're covered."

"Thanks for the pep talk." Kinski smirked.

"Anytime."

Crazy Jack Keenan was as worried as Kinski about the setup. They were heading into occupied territory to hook up with a resistance movement of unknown quality and quantity. For all he knew, they could be aided by six underage farm workers in the possession of a radio. Still, if there was a shot at kicking the FSE in the shins, hard, in France, it was a shot the Marauders had to take.

In his arms he cradled a Barrett M-82, .50-caliber semiautomatic rifle. He figured it might come in handy; at thirty-five pounds, it was something only he could handle. It was a perfect sniper's rifle, and, heading into darkness, toward *more* darkness, he figured he'd volunteer for point duty and keep his comrades covered while they searched for the members of Free France.

After all, they couldn't land on shore rocking and rolling with their automatics and attracting attention, now could they? Jack absentmindedly stroked the thirty-seven-inch barrel, pushing back memories of friends and family long gone.

He had frequent bouts with depression. He had found only one way to hold them at bay. Fight, and fight hard. Do the dance of death. After all, what was the quantum universe but one big dance? If all matter and consciousness were composed of quantum waves, it required rhythm . . . for all waves required rhythmic movement.

He caught himself staring at the ocean waves outside and chuckled to himself. "Your problem, Jack," he told himself, "is that you're too damned complicated."

He climbed up to the helm. "How're we doing?"

Bidoff squinted into the murk before the boat. "Should be at the drop-off point in about ten minutes."

"Any sign of trouble?"

"Son, in this fog there's no sign of *anything*."

Jack returned below and faced his companions. "All right, guys. Let's load up the rafts and get ready to move out."

The three other Marauders nodded. Mamudi said a silent prayer to Muhammad, said to be "Prophet when Adam was still between water and clay." He then popped in his special glass eye, one bearing the green frog emblem of the SEALs.

Buddha Chan gave his gold shooter's glasses one last wipe, cursing the dampness around him, which constantly caused the suckers to fog up. Kinski combed his hair, also cursing the rising damp. He was losing his wave.

The four men emerged on deck.

"It's cold as hell up here," Kinski groused. "Even with the wet suits on."

Buddha began stripping off the outer layer of protective clothing he wore over his wet suit. "Things are going to get a lot colder right about now."

The four men disrobed and stood in the fog, clad only in their seal-black wet suits.

"Let's get the lead out," Jack muttered.

The men placed their weaponry in the two rubber rafts hanging on each side of the boat. They were black and heavy-duty and could house four men apiece. Crazy Jack figured it would be more prudent to split up in a pair of rafts for the landing, just in case anything got a little fugazi.

The boat purred to a stop about a half mile from shore. Bidoff killed the motor. "This is it, gents," he whispered, walking out onto the deck. "Good luck and God's speed."

"Thanks, Bidoff," Kinski said with a smile.

Buddha Chan squinted through his shooter's glasses, gazing out to where the shore should be. "Jack?" he whispered.

"Yeah, Buddha?"

Chan continued to stare at the shoreline. It was nothing more than a faint outline in the drifting fog. "The beach—there's movement there."

Jack squinted at the proposed LZ. He caught a slight glimmer of light. He vaguely made out the outline of a six-by, parked near the rocky shore.

"Kinski, Freddie, up here," he called.

All four Marauders scanned the beachhead. "They can't be *that* unprofessional," Kinski hissed, "could they?"

"Bidoff," Jack said, his voice tinged with tension, "crank up the engines and get us the hell out of here."

Ka-thump.

The four Marauders knew it was too late. "Christ," Kinski hissed, "incoming."

"Get to the rafts!" Mamudi yelled. "We've got ourselves a friggin' number-ten situation here."

"Captain Bidoff, get down!" Chan yelled as the first shell hit the water with a resounding *whooosh*.

A titanic plume of water cascaded upward, spraying the boat and its inhabitants with a sheet of fouled water.

"What the hell?" Bidoff bellowed, running forward to the helm.

Jack looked over his shoulder. The shoreline seemed to light up with small, feral, glowing eyes.

"They're rocking and rolling!" Jack yelled.

He dived onto the deck as round after round of machine-gun fire strafed the boat.

"Shit," he muttered, crawling back to his already supine companions.

"I love it when we plan ahead," Kinski said, rolling over on his side. "And as always, our key element here is always the crucial one of *surprise*."

"Kinski . . ." Buddha Chan began.

"We have to get off the boat," Mamudi stated.

"Nice trick," Kinski said. "I always wanted to know how to levitate. You got time for a quick lesson?"

Kathump! Whoooosh!

The sea directly before the boat exploded with a roar, sending Bidoff tumbling ass backward off the bridge. The tall man struggled to his feet. He began to run forward when the shore was once again illuminated by countless points of light.

Jack inhaled as the old skipper's body was caught by round after round of screaming lead.

Bidoff's wiry body began to go to pieces, literally. The old man didn't have the time to utter a cry. Chunk after chunk of flesh was ripped away from his frame for what seemed an eternity. The dissolving process offered by the rounds was merciless. Bidoff's body jerked and bucked, kept vertical by the sheer ferocity of the fusillade.

Then, suddenly, the guns were silent.

Bidoff's long-dead form collapsed into a heap on the deck, over half of his body torn off its skeleton.

"Those boys aren't playing around," Kinski said, shaken by the sudden carnage. "Those aren't soldiers. Those are fucking *butchers*."

"This is it," Jack hissed. "Kinski! You and I are in raft one. Buddha! Mamudi! Hit raft number two on the count of three. One, two . . ."

The four men lurched into sprinter's position.

"Three!"

They split up into two teams and ran aft. Buddha Chan executed a double somersault into his appointed raft, Mamudi dogging his heels. Mamudi produced his stilletto and sliced through the winch ropes, allowing the raft to plunge down into dark, foreboding sea.

The guns from the shore opened up again as Jack and Kinski sliced their winch rope.

Kinski dived into the raft.

Jack hit the deck.

The raft didn't drop.

Instead it lurched to its right side, sending half of the weaponry tumbling down into the sea.

"What the . . . ?" Kinski yelled.

Jack curled himself into the fetal position as he watched the wooden deck splinter and explode around him. He raised his arms over his eyes, trying to protect them from slivers. He glanced upward. The top of the winch had been shot apart, the rope was sandwiched securely between two shattered pieces of pole.

"The fucker is jammed!" Jack bellowed.

Jack made an attempt for the pole. The bullets continued to singe the air around him. Kinski climbed out of the raft and scrambled back onto the deck.

"Get in the raft, Jack!"

"It's not going anywhere, unless we cut that line!"

"I can get up there. I'm lighter than you are. Besides, I'm a trained athlete." Kinski grinned.

"Since when?"

"Well, I always wanted to join the circus," Kinski said, turning his back on Jack and shinnying up the main pole of the winch.

"Kinski!" Jack yelled.

Another hail of bullets from the shore sliced into the dangling life raft, ripping it to shreds.

"Kinski," Jack called, "get down! It doesn't matter anymore!"

Kinski glanced downward as the last shards of the raft hit the angry ocean.

Kathump. Whoooooosh.

"Kinski!" Jack screamed as the ship's bridge disintegrated in a blinding combination of smoke and flame.

Jack's body found itself clutched by the concussion and smashed into the back railing of the boat. He heard something snap as he made contact with the metal.

Before him was nothing more than sea and flame. He felt the boat tilt ominously port side. He began to roll across the deck, attempting to claw his way to a stop, his bleeding fingers digging into the shredded deck.

He gazed upward. Kinski was still clutching the ruptured wooden pole. It was beginning to snap in two. Kinski was slowly being lowered into the inferno on deck.

"Kinski!" Jack roared, staggering to his feet. "Don't you dare, you son of a bitch!"

Jack charged toward the flames like a maddened bull elephant. "You hang on, goddamm it."

Kinski stared down at Jack, a faint smile on his lips. He raised his right hand, first saluting Jack, then adjusting his hair.

Kathump. Whoooosh.

Jack froze in his tracks. His head felt like it was entering critical meltdown status. He didn't hear the explosion, he was part of it. Senses reeling, Jack found himself airborne.

Large shards of wood tumbled through space all around him. He grasped and tore at the air. There was nothing he could do to save himself.

Sea and flame were one now, the ship's fuel igniting from the last rocket.

He felt himself falling, falling.

Kinski! his mind screamed in silence.

Around him: heat. Fire above. Fire below. Covering his face with his hands, he attempted to inhale a harsh, burning, lungful of air. He hit the water with a thud.

His body ached. He swam deeper, deeper. Above him, the ocean was afire.

Large hunks of the ship slowly began their inevitable passage to the sea floor.

Swimming furiously under water, away from the hellish fuel spill and the sinking debris, Jack spotted the slowly descending outline of the winch pole.

There was no sign of Kinski.

His lungs bursting, his consciousness fading, Jack continued to will his mighty arms and legs to pump.

He glanced upward. No sign of flames. Curling his body as if to catch a long fly ball, Jack sprung up toward the surface.

His hands clawed and pushed back the sea. His legs

churned furiously. His face finally smashed through the whitecapped water. He took a deep breath, paddling furiously. His nostrils flared, assaulted by the smell of fumes and death.

Slowly, laboriously, he began swimming out to sea. He'd rather drown like a rat than get shot down like a dog.

After a few dozen strokes he felt a hand grip him from the back of the neck.

He spun round in mid-stroke and stared up at the face of Buddha Chan.

Somehow, through some miracle, Chan and Mamudi had managed to get their raft clear of the boat before the final rocket took its toll.

"Easy now, Jack," Buddha said, sliding a chunky hand under Jack's armpit. "Easy does it."

Buddha braced his rotund body and yanked Jack's nearly lifeless form out of the still simmering sea. Mamudi remained motionless on the other side of the raft as Chan gently placed Jack down on the raft's bottom.

Jack sputtered and shivered, shaking his head from side to side, as if to refocus on reality.

"We thought you were gone for sure, Jack." Chan smiled.

"That makes the two of us," Jack said, slowly assuming a sitting position. "Kinski?"

Mamudi spoke for the first time. His voice was low, almost monotone. "No sign of him."

Buddah rested a hand on Jack's left shoulder. "The last we saw of him, he was high atop the winch."

"Yeah." Jack grinned. "Fixing his hair."

Mamudi slowly faced Jack. "There's no way he could have survived that, Jack," he said softly. "We saw the pole fall toward the flames. I'm sure he's sitting with God now, one of his forty *abdal*, forty saints."

"What the hell are you babbling about?" Jack groused. "Let's go back and look for him!"

"There's no way he could have survived," Mamudi stated flatly.

"The hell there isn't!" Jack growled. "Goddamm it, *I* survived!"

Mamudi offered a sad smile. "But you have the body of a

bull, my friend. Kinski had the heart of a lion but the body of
a deer."

"Don't give me any Bambi shit," Jack said. "We're going
back for him."

"We have the mission to think about," Buddha pointed out.

"Yeah, well, this mission is working out really well right
about now, isn't it?" Jack said, making a move toward one of
the raft's two paddles. "I say we have a better chance of suc-
cess with four of us, not three."

He wrapped a bleeding hand around a paddle and clenched
it, bearlike.

"Now," he said, staring at Freddie Mamudi, "anyone who
doesn't want to go back for Kinski can take me on right now."

Mamudi raised a finger to his zipper scar and scratched it
thoughtfully. "We all are experiencing loss, Jack. In my reli-
gion even God was lonely. That is why he created the world."

"If you don't shut up, I'm going to take out your other
eye," Jack said, simmering.

Buddha Chan sighed and, with hummingbird speed, raised
his right hand and delivered a stultifying karate chop to the
back of Jack's neck.

Jack pitched forward immediately, still clutching the paddle.

Buddha crawled forward, hovering above the prone titan
like a protective angel. He gently removed the paddle from
Jack's hand, glancing up at Freddie Mamudi. "He's better off
resting awhile, anyhow. He'll probably feel a lot better after a
good night's sleep."

Mamudi glanced at the floating debris a half mile away.
"What could have gone wrong?"

"Name something." Chan shrugged. "There could be an
informant in the ranks of Free France. Someone could have
cracked under pressure. Gremlins? I don't know."

Mamudi nodded, taking the other paddle. "Well, now
where to?"

Buddha Chan reached down into a small SP pack. "Well,
we can't try Le Havre again, that's for sure. I don't enjoy
playing sitting duck to a bunch of hard-core rock and rollers."

He glanced over his shoulder. "There's a sea town, Fecamp, north of here. I guess it's time to put some elbow grease into it."

"Do you think we'll still be able to rendezvous with our contact?"

"I don't know how we're going to find each other," Buddha Chan said. "I *do* know how we're going to find the FSE, thought—by just looking over our shoulders."

Mamudi grinned. "So we improvise?"

Buddha returned the smile. "We improvise."

Mamudi nodded. Both men began to paddle deeper into the fog, deeper into the unknown.

On shore, Jean Gaillac watched the last of his troops climb back aboard the flatbed trucks. Not bad for a bunch of foreigners, he thought. Man, what he could do with them out in the field. He could triple the amount of perks he encountered.

With troops like that, maybe he could even make Robespierre "disappear."

He was growing tired of taking orders from the slimy little bastard. He wondered what it would take to cause insurrection in the FSE ranks.

He heard a few of the men speaking German, and his blood ran cold.

I'm not a Frenchman, he thought, turning his back on them. *Don't hold grudges. You weren't even born back then. That was your father's problem, the fool. Let bygones be bygones. We're just one big happy family now.*

He faced the sea and raised a pair of binoculars to his eyes.

The last traces of the boat were just about all burned out now. The fuel slick continued to be caressed by tiny tongues of flame.

He glanced to the right of the wreckage, and then to the left. No sign of survivors.

He had seen the bodies blow into the air. He had been surprised. The invasion force had consisted of just a few men. He chuckled to himself. They were professionals. He was just a street tough. He had taken them out, though. His heart raced. He was beginning to feel proud of his accomplishment.

He lowered the glasses and proffered a long, jagged smile. "Gotcha," he whispered.

Ignoring the two flatbed trucks of imported troops, he walked past them and climbed into his jeep. He aimed the jeep for Paris. If he floored it, he'd reach the city by dawn.

Thanks be to God that the whorehouses were twenty-four-hour operations.

FIVE

Low-hanging clouds slithered between the steeples of London's proudest, oldest buildings. The sun dared not shine on this day.

Inside his office, King Shatterhand poured himself another glass of Scotch. This was a day for drinking. This was a day for remembering. Most of all, this was a day for mourning.

His console buzzed. He smashed his steel-studded stump down on it, smashing the plastic machine.

"Shit," he hissed.

A startled woman named Cheryl skittered into his den. "Your Highness, Captain Boyle from Scotland Yard is here."

"Send him in," Shatterhand mumbled.

He stared at the two typewritten pages lying on his desktop and muttered every dark oath a true Scot had ever overheard at a local pub.

A dapper man with a waxed mustache and a hastily combed headful of straw-blond hair marched into the room. "Your Highness?"

"Can it, Billy," Shatterhand said. "We go back too long a time."

"That we do, Willis," Boyle said, sliding into a chair.

"You've seen this?" Shatterhand asked.

"That I have." Boyle nodded sadly.

"Why wasn't I informed of this earlier?"

"There was a problem with radio communications, Willis," Boyle said. "The FSE is jamming us very vigorously."

"Oh, fine. Just fine." Shatterhand said, pouring himself another drink. "Have a snootful?"

"No thanks. I'm on duty," Boyle replied.

"So am I, although I don't know for how much longer." Shatterhand sighed, gazing at the reports.

"At eleven P.M., a radio report was issued by Free France," he intoned, "advising us to abort our mission. No reason given. The report didn't show up on my desk until two A.M."

"We had a hard time making it out, Willis," Boyle offered.

"Goddamm it, Billy!" Shatterhand said, pounding his hand into his desktop so hard the studded glove embedded itself into the wood. "I sent four men out to their deaths!"

"You can't be sure of that, Willis," Boyle injected.

"Oh, but I can," Shatterhand replied. "I take it you haven't seen the second report."

"That I haven't," Boyle admitted. "We had a murder in the Chelsea district last night. Reportedly an FSE supporter. A mob appeared at his door and . . . well, you know how bad things can get very quickly."

"Take a look at it," Shatterhand said, tossing the paper in the policeman's direction.

Boyle read the report. "I can't believe it."

Shatterhand raised his massive form and leaned over his desk, snatching back the typewritten report. "Believe it. This arrived at five A.M. One of your toadies delivered it. It's the last transmission we received from Free France before all communication ceased."

He gazed, bleary-eyed, at the report. "'Invasion force attacked. Debris and body parts found on shore. No sign of survivors. Regrets. We cannot continue transmitting much longer. The FSE . . .'"

Shatterhand put the paper down. "And that, my friend, is that."

"I don't understand," Boyle said. "Surely we can send in our own men."

"Our men aren't ready to take on the FSE abroad yet. They're mere pups in terms of military skills. The Marauders were our only hope. Now that they're gone, not only can't I avenge their deaths, but also I may not even be able to defend our country for the next six months!"

Boyle sank lower in his chair. "What would you like me to do?"

"Word is bound to leak out on this," Shatterhand said. "So, to avoid rumors, I'll issue a public statement. Double the amount of street patrols. I don't know how the populace will react to this. The Marauders were larger-than-life figures to them, everybody's best friends. I know they were mine."

He poured himself another drink. "I stay up all night and nobody contacts me about this. I could have saved their lives if I had known. I could have contacted that goddamn ship. Turned them around. Try again tomorrow. Or the day after tomorrow. But now . . . ?"

"It's not your fault, Willis," Boyle stated.

"The hell it isn't," Shatterhand said, guzzling from his glass. "Contact the prime minister. Tell him I want him ready to stand by me when I address the people. I want all networks and radio stations primed for noon today. I want the prime minister to declare tomorrow a day of national mourning."

"What about the United States' president?" Boyle asked.

"I'll call him myself," Shatterhand said. "He's a distant cousin of mine . . . I'd like to tell him myself."

Shatterhand's bearded chin lowered itself down upon his chest. "Oh, almighty God. This is all my fault. It was me who went to America for support, who caused these gallant lads to be brought together, who sent them out on this mission."

He slowly lifted his head. "And now it is me who must tell the world they were killed in action."

He poured himself a drink and hoisted it toward the ornate ceiling in the palace office. "The Marauders are *dead*. Long live the Marauders."

He downed his drink and stared at Boyle.

Boyle got to his feet in a long, languid motion. "Perhaps, Willis, I will have a drink, after all."

SIX

Buddha Chan and Mamudi paddled the small raft toward shore. There was no sign of a town. No sign of civilization. The sun tried, in vain, to break through the intrusive gloom above their heads. Somewhere in the distance, a lone sea gull cried.

Crazy Jack Keenan still lay sprawled at the bottom of the raft.

"I don't think we've reached our destination," Mamudi surmised.

"We'll land here," Buddha Chan replied, "set up a temporary base camp. I don't want to be paddling around here in broad daylight."

"I wouldn't call this daylight," Mamudi said, staring at the solid gray sky above him.

"Too risky," Chan replied. "We'll stow the raft and set out again tonight."

Mamudi glanced up once more. "The sun is starting to break through."

"Paddle as you've never paddled before, Popeye," Buddha Chan said with a grunt.

"I resemble that remark," Mamudi said, double-timing his paddling.

The black raft crashed ashore on a strip of sandy, rocky beach.

Buddha Chan and Mamudi leapt out of the raft, still clad in their wet suits and, waist-deep in water, pulled the rubber craft onto solid ground.

Jack stirred. "Where the hell? What the hell?"

"Shhhh," Buddha Chan said. "You're still weak."

"The hell I am, you little gook!" Jack bellowed, leaping out of the raft and planting his Brobdingnagian feet on the sand. "You coldcocked me."

"You were delirious." Buddha Chan smiled, slightly fearful of Jack's towering frame.

"I'll give you delirious—"

"Jack! Buddha!" Mamudi cautioned. "We have more serious affairs to attend to. It is written—"

"Stow it," Jack and Buddha Chan said in unison.

The short Mongol and the towering half Irish, half Ukrainian giant glanced at each other. They both began laughing.

"Come on," Jack said. "Let's get this raft stowed."

"Glad to have you back, Jack," Mamudi said, grabbing his portion of the raft and dragging it, with his two compatriots, toward the rocks.

The sun began to burst through the clouds. "And not a moment too soon," Buddha Chan said.

The trio continued to drag the battered black raft over the pebble-strewn sand, the morning sun now glaring down on them.

Without warning the sun was blotted out.

The three Marauders looked up.

Towering above them was a massive, round figure, clenched fists firmly placed on hips.

Buddha Chan did a double take. It surely was his namesake. Had he died and gone on to another world?

Jack made a move to grab a rifle from the raft. He heard several clicking sounds from all around him.

"I wouldn't try it, Yank" came a vaguely female voice from the shadow-shape above them.

Jack froze. Then he slowly withdrew his hand.

The three Marauders gazed up at the figure in silence. The gigantic creature ambled down the shoreline.

"We were wondering when you'd finally have the sense to go ashore," it said.

The figure stepped into the sunlight. It was a woman. A very, very big woman—large and wide, almond eyes, curly black hair, wearing peasant garb. She didn't seem exceedingly young, nor did she seem old. In truth, she seemed a mass of ageless flesh.

She smiled at the three men. Her teeth were perfect. "You are the Marauders?"

"We are," Buddha Chan answered.

"I thought there'd be more of you," the woman said.

"There *were*," Jack said bitterly.

The woman's cherubic face formed a sorrowful mask. "Ah" was all she said, shaking her double-chinned head up and down. "I understand."

She extended a beefy hand. "I am Marie Marrette. Your contact?"

Mamudi regarded her in silence. Jack took her hand and pumped it. "Free France?"

"That's the rumor," she replied, shrugging her shoulders. "For the record, ah, who can tell?"

Jack tried to smile. He instinctively liked this woman. Yet he couldn't forget Kinski's last stand on the boat. He tried to push the mental portrait from his mind. "I'm Captain Jack Keenan. My friends call me Crazy Jack."

Marie smiled. "All Americans are crazy."

Buddha Chan slid his shooter's glasses to the tip of his nose and peered out at Marie from above them. "Believe me, he's crazier than most."

Jack waved a blood-encrusted hand at the others. "And this is Sergeant Winston S. Chan and CPO Farouz Mamudi. He's just Freddie to us."

Buddha Chan also shook her hand. "What . . . happened last night?"

"We tried to warn you," Marie explained. "One of our younger members was captured. Tortured and killed, apparently. He betrayed you and led the FSE to our main communications base. It was near Le Havre, on the coastline. It's easier to reach Britain when you are merely transmitting across the Channel. We lost fourteen men last night, and our transmitter. We managed to get most of the message out before the grenades hit but . . ."

"There's no way of contacting Britain?" Jack asked.

"As of now, no," Marie said.

"Great," Jack muttered. "Then, as of now, for all they know, we're dead."

"Perhaps that's all for the better." Marie smiled, exposing dimples big enough to stick a finger into. "If they think you're dead and gone, then the FSE thinks you're dead and gone. Nobody attempts to kill the dead, eh?"

"I like the way you think, Marie." Buddha Chan chuckled, wiping the sand from his shooter's glasses.

"Thank you." Marie nodded. "Now let's get you all the hell out of here. When the fog breaks up, you're going to stand out like raisins on oatmeal out here on the beach."

She raised a beefy arm. Two dozen young men, armed with rifles, descended from behind the rocks. Jack and Buddha Chan exchanged startled looks.

Marie smiled. "We knew you were going to be attacked, so we had spotters all along the coast. Once we knew you survived . . ."

"Not all of us," Jack muttered.

". . . we traced your route. You fellows do well in the sea. There aren't many men who can maneuver a raft like that."

She turned her back on the men and waddled toward the small road running along the shoreline. "Come on now. Let's get your out of those silly suits and into some *real* clothes. My men will bring along your weapons and destroy your raft."

Mamudi stood silently, watching the mountainous woman amble forward. She was the largest, most intriguing woman he had ever seen.

He reached into a pouch firmly attached to his wet suit and produced a new glass eye. Popping out his SEAL orb, he quickly affixed his newest choice for eyeballing in place.

In the center of the iris was a large heart.

He smiled to himself, his heart skipping a beat.

He was in love. He knew it.

Marie continued to waddle uphill. Mamudi continued to stare, transfixed.

This would be his next wife.

SEVEN

The naked man ran through the bushes, cursing each time his body encountered a thorn or his feet stumbled over a sharp stone. Far in the distance he saw a farmhouse, replete with barn. If he could make it to the barn, he'd figure out how to get himself out of this predicament.

He stared at the buildings for what seemed like hours. In reality it was only minutes.

Then he heard an ominous click.

He spun around to face a uniformed police officer, pistol drawn.

Aimed at his forehead.

"You will excuse me," the policeman said, "but I had a report of a man, *au naturel*, lurking in the woods. I could not believe it myself, of course. We are too civilized a country for that. But then, I thought, since the last war, times are strange. So I decided to investigate the reports myself. And now, much to my surprise, I find you."

The naked man slid his hands down in order to cover his private parts. He offered a shy, embarrassed grin.

The policeman did not return it. "I am Inspector Lechat of Normandy province."

The nude man blinked.

"And your name?" Lechat asked, wheedling.

The man muttered something in Polish.

"Again?" Lechat asked.

The nude man attempted a grin. "Kinski," he replied. "Petrovich Kinski."

"Aha." The inspector sighed, slowing down his words as if

to make them more understandable. "You . . . are . . . not . . . French?"

"Petrovich Kinski."

Lechat thought hard. He switched languages.

"Do . . . you . . . speak . . . English?"

Kinski grinned wide. "A . . . leedle . . . yes."

"Where . . . are . . . you . . . from?"

"Poland."

Lechat nodded. "Good. *Très bien*. Why . . . are . . . you . . . uh . . . without—what is the word?—apparel?"

"Robbers surprised me. Robbed me. Left me for dead."

Kinski displayed a bullet graze on his thigh. "They took everything. *Everything*."

Lechat seemed to consider this fact. "Ah, *oui*, I mean, yes. Times are difficult. Strange things happen all the time. What is your profession?"

"Pro-fes-sion?"

"What is it you do?"

"I was . . . a soldier once. Now I wander," Kinski said, laying on his broken English with a verbal trowel.

Lechat grinned. "Well, that is very good. Very good indeed."

Kinski nodded dumbly. "It *is*?"

"Oh, *oui*. Yes. There are some nearby who have the use of a good soldier. Come. Come back with me to my car. We will give you a blanket. Take you back to my headquarters."

"Hungry," Kinski muttered.

"But of course! We will feed you and clothe you as well. We will treat you like a soldier. A *real* soldier."

"Thank you."

"Don't mention it. It is the least I can do for a military man. I was in the military myself, you know."

"No."

"Oh, *oui*. Yes. Part of the U.N. peace keeping force in Israel. But that was a long time ago."

"Yes."

"Come, my compatriot," Lechat said, twisting his bulldog visage into the semblance of a smile. "Let us go. I will introduce you to a man who is in dire need of experienced men to work with."

"What man is this?" Kinski asked, affixing a stupefied expression to his face.

"A fellow named Gaillac. I'm sure you two will get along well. He is also a soldier and a wanderer, in his own way."

The short, muscular policeman took Kinski by the wrist and led him out of the bushes.

From far below, on the farm, two women screamed.

"Don't let it bother you, my friend." Lechat shrugged. "They have seen naked men before. They are just trying to impress me. I am not impressed."

Kinski nodded.

"Those brigands who attacked you," Lechat continued, "they were probably part of Free France. They consider themselves patriots, but in reality they are nothing but fools. They don't realize what a good thing they have. Things could be much worse here in France. We survived a nuclear war and we still have a government. Yet they complain. Silly, eh?"

Kinski blinked. "Silly, yes."

"You have heard, of course, of the FSE?"

"Of course."

"Well, I believe it's time you joined their ranks. It's the only way to survive safely, you know. Had you been a member of the FSE, this misfortune never would have befallen you. There is strength in numbers, don't you see? The world is a dangerous place."

Kinski rolled his eyes heavenward. Out of the frying pan and into the fire.

He had been in number-ten situations before . . .

But he had never been in a number-ten squared.

He hoped that Jack, Buddha Chan, and Mamudi had survived the attack. If not, he was the only foreign invasion force to be found this side of the English Channel.

EIGHT

Marie managed to find clothing that fit Jack, Buddha Chan, and Mamudi . . . approximately. The sleeves of Jack's tunic ended long before his arms did. Buddha had trouble buttoning his shirt over his round, barrel chest. Mamudi? What did he care? He had finally found the warrior princess of his dreams.

Marie sat them at a table in a farmhouse not far from Le Havre, feeding them bread and bowls of heavily creamed coffee.

She watched the trio eat in silence. Mamudi felt obliged to begin his courtship. The best he could muster was "What's a nice girl like you—" He stopped, embarrassed.

"Doing in a movement like this?" Marie laughed. "My God, you Americans don't change. My grandmother told me about lines like that used after the Second World War. Only then the GIs used to hand out chocolate and nylons."

Jack and Buddha Chan smiled, suddenly finding their coffee very interesting.

"I lived on a farm in the north country," Marie explained, chewing on a hunk of crusty bread. "Suddenly there was no farm. The FSE took over. My family resisted. Suddenly there was no family. I am under thirty and a woman. Only two choices there: cathouses or hard labor. Obviously I am not cathouse material."

"That's not true!" Mamudi blurted. "I mean, no, you're not, but you're very attractive."

"Don't flatter me, Mr. Mamudi. I know you only have one good eye. So I'm used to hard labor. I've done it all my life, but *mon Dieu*, I was not about to toil for the oppressors, eh? I

49

came south. Met a fellow named Gerard. This is his farm—or *was*. He was part of the Resistance."

"What happened to Gerard?" Jack asked.

"He 'disappeared' shortly after the mandates took effect," Marie said wistfully. "But that's the way things are these days. We want to change that."

"We'll change it," Jack vowed.

Buddha Chan took a sip of coffee. "Where's your base of operations?"

"You're sitting in part of it." Marie smiled, waving her hand at the farmhouse around her.

"This farm?" Jack gulped. "But how? Isn't it dangerous being so close to a major city like Le Havre?"

"Yes and no," Marie explained. "Yes, because we *are* close to regular FSE patrols and routines. No, because it's necessary for us to monitor their movements. We are also well protected. We run a good farm here. We are productive. We dutifully turn over most of our yield to the FSE. And at a time when many farmers are holding back, this places us beyond reproach."

"An excellent tactic," Mamudi said. "I like your approach."

"Do you have weaponry?" Jack asked.

Marie smiled. "Come, I'll show you."

She led the three men from the kitchen out into the open. Several dozen men toiled in the fields. Inside the barn, cows were in the process of being milked. Marie motioned the Marauders trio to the far end of the barn.

Glancing to and fro, she reached down under the straw-laden floor and lifted a large trapdoor. At the base of the door was a set of sturdy wooden stairs leading downward. "This way," she said, pointing. "Be careful descending. The ladder is steep. I'd hate to have you break your necks on a step."

Crazy Jack and Buddha Chan took to the stairs. Marie motioned for Mamudi to follow. Mamudi pushed his hair away from his zipper scar. "After *you*, my dear lady."

"Americans," Marie muttered, waddling down the stairs. Mamudi smiled and followed.

In the darkness below the barn, Marie extended a pudgy hand and flicked on a light switch. The Marauders trio gasped as several fluorescent lights fluttered to life. They found themselves in an underground den roughly fifty by fifty. Stacked against a wall were crates of weaponry.

Jack walked over to the crates, whistling through his teeth. "M-1s, M-60s, a few M-16s, AK-47s! Where the hell did you get this stuff?"

"It was difficult"—Marie chuckled—"let me tell you. When we first heard rumors of an English king being put on the throne with the help of Americans, our hopes soared. We have a few former military men in our ranks, a few politicians, a few people who once worked with Interpol. They knew where arms were kept near our military bases. Hidden from the public. France, before the war, didn't want to seem too *aggressive*, you see. There were many covert operations that went on in those days, like the blowing-up of the Greenpeace ship. One of our sources say that was government-sanctioned. Nobody ever admitted it, though.

"And then it turns out your government helped as well. Several of your higher-ups used Marseilles as a port of call for their own private agendas. Trading drug money for arms sent everywhere, from Northern Ireland to Nicaragua. Even though your then president outlawed such actions, he conveniently got something in his eye when he noticed some of his cabinet members taking sides.

"Then the war came, and many of Marseilles' more colorful characters found themselves, shall we say, overstocked? We traded them food for guns. Then all trading stopped. The mandates were issued. Since then it has been difficult to find new weaponry. On occasion we are lucky. More often than not, we have to be very, very cautious. That, in turn, leads to coming up dry."

"You are truly magnificent." Mamudi grinned.

"Right." Marie shrugged.

"How did you ever manage to build this place?" Buddha Chan asked. "Without getting caught, I mean."

"We didn't," Marie replied. "It was built by the French resistance during the Second World War. There are many such places throughout the country. They were used as meeting places, as hideouts for political refugees, for storage of whatever was necessary to survive during the Nazi occupation."

She walked over to a large map near the wall. "We are using such safe places here, all along the Seine. There are

Free France strongholds near Elbeuf, Vernon, Gennevillers, Créteil, and Evry. Those are the ones I am sure of in this area."

"Why haven't you started any operations on your own?" Jack asked. "You've had the time."

"But not the manpower," Marie said. "Many joined our ranks after the mandates were passed. In effect, the FSE *drove* them to us. We had planned to allow our ranks to grow, and then to start hit-and-run strikes all over the nation. That dream came to an end four months ago when activities of the Federated enforcers increased."

"Goon squads," Buddha Chan said, nodding his rotund head.

"They effectively sectioned off different areas of the country, making it hard for us, for instance, to contact groups in the Gascogne area or Bretagne. We know they are out there, but we simply cannot reach them. When we established communications with Britain, we asked for help immediately. We thought that if we could make things hot for the FSE here, word would spread. The others would spring to action."

"And soon the entire country would be pinpricked with incidents." Mamudi grinned. "Excellent strategy, the essence of guerrilla work."

Marie ignored him, continuing to look at the map. "Frankly we hoped there were more of you. However, British Intelligence told us how you instigated the overthrow of the FSE in Scotland, England, and Ireland. We hope you will prove equally as adept in France.

"Things are getting very, very bad. Half of the public buildings in Paris are being used either as garrisons or prisons. Many of our key leaders have been herded there, publicly and regularly executed by Eastern European FSE troops. Our less important members or supporters are slaughtered wherever they are found."

Jack stared at the map. "Paris is a military encampment now?"

"Yes," Marie said sadly. "All of her citizens work for the FSE occupation. If they fall behind in their quotas, it's into jail for them."

Buddha Chan walked over to the map. "Interesting, isn't it, Jack, how the Seine would take us straight into the city?"

"What are you saying?" Mamudi said, turning his attention from the corpulent object of his affection. His face brightened. "Miss Marrette, does the FSE use the Seine much? For transporting troops or supplies?"

"Oh, no," Marie answered. "It's too slow for them. They prefer to travel the highways in packs as a show of strength to civilians."

Crazy Jack smiled at his two comrades. "Are we in agreement, then?"

Buddha Chan chuckled, gleefully rubbing the top of his bald head. "It *would* be a very visible gesture."

Mamudi nodded. "It certainly would shake up the FSE."

Marie's face formed an inquisitive look. "Just what are you talking about?"

Jack turned to her. "We're going to travel up the Seine and rally your supporters at all your strongholds."

"And then?" Marie asked.

"We're going to liberate Paris," Crazy Jack said.

NINE

Kinski sat in the passenger's seat of the small police sedan and watched the French countryside zip by his window. The closer the sedan got to Paris, the more conspicuous were the FSE troops, both foreign and local.

Behind the wheel, Lechat peppered Kinski with questions. "How is it, my friend, that you have managed to stay alive on your own all these years?"

"I'm a survivor," Kinski said truthfully.

"Ah, yes. That is a must in today's world. We are all survivors. But, I mean, *surely* your homeland is a stronghold of the FSE."

"It is." Kinski nodded.

"But you never felt the need or the desire to join their ranks?"

"I did not."

"And why is that, exactly?"

"To be honest, Inspector, following the last war, I grew disgusted with government, *all* government. It was a needless war. Many of my compatriots died. Innocent citizens. Poland is much closer to Russia than France. The aftereffects were much more drastic."

"Ah" was all Lechat could muster for a reply.

Kinski smiled to himself. He could still lie with the best of them. Before the war, he had earned the nickname Silver Tongue, for his ability to tell the damnedest stories to his commanders and various bureaucrats and, through his apparent sincerity, get them to believe him. If it hadn't been for his yarn-spinning skills, he probably would have been bounced out of the Air Force years ago. He had been, and still was, a man who resented dinosaur authority. He liked to party hearty and often. A good lie could cover his tracks.

Now it had to save his life. He had to get a message to Shatterhand and report on the situation. He had to contact Free France. How? He didn't know. He'd think of something.

"We are nearing Paris," Lechat said.

Kinski passively stared out the windshield of the white sedan. In the distance he could see the majesty of the Eiffel Tower. Perhaps, another time, the sight would have filled him with awe. Today it only filled him with dread.

"If I know our Jean Gaillac," Lechat said with a grin, "he will be in the Fisted Glove."

"What's the Fisted Glove?"

"A saloon, and so much more," Lechat replied with a wink. "It is very popular with the FSE men."

Kinski nodded, sharpening his silver tongue.

The Fisted Glove was an ornate dive on the once prosperous Right Bank of Paris. Once frequented by business tycoons and wealthy tourists in its former incarnation as a nightclub, it was now as rowdy as an old-fashioned roadhouse. Loud music and louder men and women, with even louder makeup, caroused there twenty-four hours a day.

For a few francs you could get a stiff drink. For a few francs more you could get a pliable woman. If you had a gun and knew how to use it, you could get both without pulling out your billfold.

Jean Gaillac sat at a round table in the back of the smoke-filled cabaret, nursing his umpteenth Scotch. The pride he had felt in his master kill the night before had worn off. The familiar feeling of numbness was returning.

He was running out of things to do in life. He had to find something new, something exciting, something kinky. Every sordid act that was possible, every atrocity imaginable, he had done, both on the battlefield and in the affordable rented bedrooms of France. He had killed, tortured, raped, stolen. He had killed bed partners as they reached orgasm.

Someone near the jukebox pushed a button. The long-dead American songstress Peggy Lee began singing "Is That All There Is?" Gaillac smiled to himself. Perhaps if he could locate some heavy artillery, he could take out a whole town while it slept. That might be good for a laugh or two.

He saw two men approach his table. One was short and stout, wore a jaunty hat tilted to one side, and had the jowls of a bulldog. The other was tall, blond, and sinewy. Despite the shabby, baggy clothing he wore, the stranger exuded a feeling of strength and dignity.

The hair on the back of Gaillac's neck began to stand on end as Inspector Lechat led Kinski over to his table.

"Lechat," Gaillac said with a nod. "Why aren't you out harassing your peasants?"

Lechat made an attempt to laugh heartily. It sounded like he had a hair ball caught deep down in his throat. "Ahaha. Today I excused myself from duties because I found a rather interesting person on my rounds. A person I think you should meet. He only speaks English, so in deference to him, let's talk so that we all will understand, eh?"

Gaillac nodded.

"Jean Gaillac? This is Petrovich Kinski, native of Poland, former soldier."

Gaillac raised his eyes to Kinski's. He regarded him in silence. Kinski did the same and slid into a chair opposite Gaillac's.

Gaillac snapped his fingers. "Bartender, another bottle."

A man on the other side of the room scurried toward the bar.

Gaillac twisted his apelike lips into a thin smile. "I hope you like Scotch."

Kinski nodded. "I have been drinking vodka since the age of ten. There is nothing more powerful than vodka."

Kinski returned the phony smile.

Lechat sat in a chair between them. "See? See? I knew you two would enjoy each other's company. Two soldiers, eh? One from the FSE and one from the Polish Army."

Gaillac stared hard at Kinski. "Polish Army?"

"Before the war."

"Why did you leave?"

"There wasn't much of an army left after the fallout hit."

"What have you been doing since then?"

"Getting as far away from there as possible."

"Any affiliations?"

"I'm a Catholic."

Gaillac found himself enjoying the game of cat and mouse. "No, I meant political."

"My father was a member of Solidarity. He was a great believer in workers' rights. He was imprisoned for it. Me? I'm a great believer in two things: myself and keeping myself alive."

Gaillac stared into the thin, blond man's lackluster eyes. There was something in there, a steellike quality he was wary of yet respected.

"But you were a good soldier. . . ."

Kinski shrugged. "I obeyed orders."

"Have you killed?"

"Many."

Gaillac ran a callused hand across his granite chin. "Would you be interested in working for the FSE?"

"If the terms are correct."

"A man in my position could simply conscript you, you know. You'd be forced to serve."

"I'd probably do a bad job."

"And why is that?"

"Because I wouldn't believe in the 'cause.'"

"But if the terms were right, you'd believe?"

"If the terms were right, it would benefit my favorite cause . . . Petrovich Kinski." Kinski found himself grinning. He was doing a pretty good snow job.

Gaillac laughed out loud. "I like your attitude, Kinski. It stinks. If I recommend you for an FSE post, I'd have to take you to my commander."

"I can handle it."

"I'm sure you can," Gaillac said, feeling the warm glow of whiskey spread inside his stomach.

"See?" Lechat said proudly. "See? Is this not a good thing I have done?"

"It may be," Gaillac said, pushing his chair against a wall filled with mirrors, paintings with glittering frames, and various knicknacks.

Lechat could not keep his lips still for a moment. He turned to Kinski. "Since the FSE strengthened its presence here a year ago it has been our own Jean who has kept the rabble in line. He is a magnificent strategist. Last night he single-han-

dedly managed to wipe out an invading force sent by the
Americans and the British."

Lechat spat on the sawdust-topped floor. "The British! I
hate them."

Kinski's stomach tightened. He glanced at Gaillac. "Impressive."

Gaillac offered a smirk as a reply. "Not really. It was a
joke. One boat. We blew them out of the water within a minute. A schoolboy could have done that."

"Any survivors?"

"Nothing but fish food left."

At that point the enfeebled bartender approached the table,
an open whiskey bottle and two glasses perched precariously
on a tray.

At the last moment, just before reaching Gaillac's party,
the old man tripped, sending the tray and its contents sailing
into space.

With lightning speed Kinski grabbed the two glasses as
they tumbled toward the floor. The tray hit Lechat in the head
and the bottle landed on its side, sending a splash of whiskey
onto Gaillac's muddied pants.

"Damn you!" he bellowed.

He reached down beside his chair and yanked up a Chinese-made AK-47 86s bullpup. The bullpup was identical to
the gun Kinski loved to use but much smaller, twenty-six
inches long instead of the usual thirty-five.

Gaillac trained the gun on the frightened man. The entire
cabaret grew silent. The men seated behind the bartender
slowly got up and moved toward the exit.

"Do you know who I am?" Gaillac asked.

"Yes, Monsieur Gaillac," the bartender replied in a hoarse
whisper.

"And yet you see fit to ridicule me?"

"It w-was an accident, monsieur," the old man said, stammering. "These old legs of mine, they do not work as well as
they used to."

"And now," Gaillac said, "they will not work at all."

He made a move to squeeze the trigger, thought better of it,
and turned to Kinski.

"Here, Petrovich," he said, tossing the gun to Kinski. "You
take care of him. Any man working for me kills my enemies."

Kinski extended his right hand and deftly caught the rifle. He got to his feet and aimed the weapon at the trembling old man. Lechat grinned and winked at Gaillac.

Kinski tried not to show his uneasiness. He had to get out of the situation. He couldn't just kill an innocent man simply to maintain his cover. The beginnings of a plan began to form in the back of his mind. It would be risky, but it was worth trying.

He swung around and trained it on a startled Gaillac. Lechat sat stunned, speechless. Gaillac's eyes widened to the size of berets.

Kinski squeezed the trigger, sending round after round of 7.62- ×39-mm ammo into the wall behind Gaillac. Mirrors smashed. Knickknacks exploded. Gaudy pictures disintegrated. Kinski continued to press the trigger firmly, slowly making a circle around Gaillac.

The disoriented Goon raised his arms over his head to protect himself from the debris tumbling down all around him.

Daylight began to show through the large chunks Kinski tore out of the wall.

When the clip was spent, Kinski calmly placed the gun in front of a seething Gaillac. He turned to the old man. "Better go now."

The bartender began to scamper away.

"Not until I say so!" Gaillac bellowed.

Lechat sat quivering in his chair. The bartender froze in his tracks.

"Why didn't you kill him?" Gaillac roared at Kinski.

Kinski slowly seated himself. "I didn't see the need."

"He is my *enemy*!"

Kinski shrugged. "He's not mine."

"I told you, any man working for me kills my enemies."

"I'm not working for you . . . yet." Kinski smiled thinly.

Gaillac was flummoxed. "I . . . I could kill you."

"No," Kinski said. "You could try."

Gaillac tilted his head from one side to the other. He saw, for the first time, the strength of the stranger's steely gaze. Unexpectedly he began to laugh.

"By God, I now see how you survived all those years wandering alone! Ha, ha! You only care about yourself!"

"In order to survive, you have to," Kinski explained.

"I'll drink to that!" Gaillac said, upending the new bottle of whiskey.

"Fortunately I still have the glasses," Kinski said, pushing the two tumblers forward.

Gaillac quickly poured three rounds. The three men raised their glasses. "To me, myself, and I," he toasted.

The three men quaffed their liquor.

Lechat was still confused. He hadn't understood the toast any more than he had understood what had just happened between the two men.

"I have done a good thing, have I not, Jean?" he asked lamely.

"A very good thing," Gaillac replied.

"A very good thing, indeed," Kinski echoed.

The bartender still stood trembling, near the table. Gaillac turned around. "Well, what are you standing there for, idiot? Get us another bottle, and be careful this time!"

Kinski added with a smile, "We're running out of walls."

TEN

The afternoon sun shone brightly on the once gay city of Paris. Gaillac sent his jeep hurtling through the former student quarter, showing Kinski the sights.

"A nice place, eh?" he asked.

Kinski glanced at the buildings around him. Most of the old hotels and homes were now occupied by FSE troops and supporters. The rest, he figured, were populated by those who opposed the FSE and were under house arrest . . . or worse.

Ahead loomed Notre Dame. Kinski stared at the top of the church. Someone had been using the fierce stone gargoyles, the guardians of the dome, for target practice.

"It's very impressive," Kinski finally said.

"I lived here before the war," Gaillac said. "Things were more relaxed then. But times change, eh?"

Kinski noted that there were very few private cars on the road, as well as little pedestrian traffic but for the odd FSE-employed office worker.

Indeed, the FSE had turned Paris into a military stronghold. It was a city under siege.

"I want you to meet my superior," Gaillac said, aiming his jeep toward the Champs-Elysées. Kinski shook his head sadly, noting the gunman placed atop the Arc de Triomphe. Snipers.

The jeep pulled up in front of an incredibly posh hotel. In spite of years of neglect—the canopy was torn, the flower boxes now filled with nothing more than dry, caked dirt—the building still gave off a feeling of majesty and power. It seemed logical that the FSE stooges would use this as their command post.

Kinski allowed himself to be led inside the large structure and taken, by elevator, to the second floor.

Armed guards were positioned along the halls.

"I've never seen so many uniforms since I left the army," Kinski said.

"That's but the half of it. There are tens of thousands like me who don't wear a uniform but are more fierce than these immigrants here." Gaillac blushed slightly. "No offense."

"None taken," Kinski replied.

Gaillac walked up to a door and swung it open. Inside, mousy Giles Robespierre looked up, in the midst of a phone conversation. He motioned the two men to sit while repeating the word *yes* over and over again, occasionally spicing things up with a clever phrase like *I understand.*

Kinski watched the well-dressed ferret wipe the sweat from his brow with a small hankie. So *this* was Giles Robespierre, Maximov's chief puppet in France. Kinski couldn't figure it. Maximov was a bear of a man, a tyrant. This pipsqueak? He looked like the "before" picture in a gymnasium's before-and-after ad.

Robespierre replaced the phone in its cradle. He scrambled to his feet and stuck a limp hand out toward Gaillac. "Congratulations, Jean. Your victory last night was impressive, indeed. We have taught both the British and the Americans a deadly lesson."

Gaillac's right paw engulfed Robespierre's tiny hand. "Yeah, right."

Gaillac motioned to Kinski. "I have a man I want you to meet. He speaks only English."

"He is an American?" Robespierre chirped in French.

"No," Gaillac replied in English, "a Pole."

"Ah, that is better. Many of our finest FSE leaders were born in the Ukraine." Giles Robespierre flashed an insincere smile at Kinski. Kinski did his best to ape it.

"Giles Robespierre," Gaillac said, droning on, "I want you to meet Petrovich Kinski. I want him working with me from now on."

Robespierre blanched. "Of course. But, Jean, you know we usually have a training period—"

"Bullshit," Jean said. "This man was a soldier. He still *is* as far as I'm concerned and he can handle a gun better than half the hayseeds you've saddled me with."

"Well—"

"Look," Gaillac said firmly. "Either he comes out with me on my next tour or you can get yourself another nursemaid for those homegrown jerks."

Robespierre gulped and nodded. He extended a hand Kinski's way. "Pleased to meet you, Mr. Kinski. Welcome to the FSE."

Kinski took the man's sweaty palm and shook it. "Thank you. I've heard a lot about you, Mr. Robespierre."

"You have?" The little man swallowed hard. "Good things, I hope."

Kinski nodded. "Oh, yeah. You hear a lot of things traveling by yourself. Giles Robespierre, the Scourge of Marseilles."

"They call me *that*?" Robespierre beamed.

"And *more*," Kinski replied, not exactly stretching the truth too much. "Guns. Drugs. Women. You were a regular retailer when it came to crime."

"Those were the days, my friend," Robespierre said, walking to the bar. "Cognac, anyone?"

"Whiskey," Gaillac answered.

"Vodka, please," Kinski replied.

Robespierre served the drinks. "I am glad you have joined us, Mr. Kinski. Jean, here, is a wonderful soldier. It will be good for him to have a companion in the field, someone he can rely on. We have a lot of the local youth in our ranks, but frankly, they are not well trained, not well seasoned. Perhaps with you and Jean working together we can flatten this insurrectionist movement in the countryside in half the time. We have but four weeks."

"Why the hurry?" Kinski asked. "And what's the big problem? The soldiers I saw in Paris today don't look like former farmhands to me, and they don't look local. Many of them seem to have been born in my homeland."

"You are very observant." Robespierre cackled. "Yes, we are in the midst of a massive troop buildup. Within a month there will be many more of our comrades from Eastern Europe arriving. That is why it is necessary for us to take a few well-trained men, couple them with our locals, and crush this rebellion."

"I'm not sure I follow you," Kinski replied.

"Me, either, Giles," Gaillac echoed. "Don't talk in riddles."

Robespierre's eyes took on a faraway look. "In a month's time we will have thousands more troops here. Plus, we will be using the airport to house no less than forty helicopters, military models replete with machine guns and sophisticated tracking equipment."

Kinski began to sweat. "That's impossible!"

"So everyone thinks," Robespierre said, chuckling. "But our East German friends can be very, very resourceful when they have to be. We raided the NATO and U.S. bases in and around West Germany and managed to acquire a good many damaged vehicles. Since our troubles began to the west, these vehicles have been being repaired and reserviced twenty-four hours a day, seven days a week. Not only are they capable of flying, but also they are capable of destroying."

The little man guzzled his drink.

Kinski tried to wheedle just a tad more information. "But what's the point?"

"Yeah," Gaillac groused. "Why bring all those foreigners in? We're doing fine."

"We *are*," Robespierre acknowledged, "but I'm afraid that in light of the recent British uprising, American intervention, and the creation of Free France, we might not be for long."

"We can handle it," Gaillac said.

"Chairman Maximov does not see it that way." Giles shrugged. "He says, and rightly so, that as long as the rabble has hope for the future, they will avoid the constraints of the present for as long as possible. As long as there is a free England, a certain element of *every* country will long for that freedom."

"So?" Gaillac answered.

"So," Giles Robespierre replied, filling his glass with more cognac, "for the next few weeks you and your new partner will be taking on assignment after assignment, every day. We want to make sure the people are not capable of shifting into a state of civil unrest after the bulk of the troops leaves France, leaves to embark on one of the most stunning victories we will ever have the privilege of relishing."

"And what's that?" Kinski asked.

"Gentlemen," Giles said, nursing his liquor. "In one month we will invade England and bring it back into the FSE fold . . . no matter the price."

ELEVEN

Kinski watched as Jean Gaillac, aided by two dozen Goons, went through the drill in the small village of Laplume, some fifty miles south of Paris.

"This is the enemy?" Kinski asked.

"Who knows?" Gaillac said. "Giles tells me to terrorize them, I terrorize them. I don't give a damn who or what they are."

Great, Kinski thought. He was definitely dealing with a being very low on the food chain.

Kinski, an AK-47 slung over his shoulder, watched as Gaillac calmly herded the villagers into four groups: older men, older women, young women, and young boys.

"What happens now?" Kinski asked.

"We kill those two groups, have fun, and make use of the other two. Happens all the time," Gaillac replied. He patted Kinski on the back. "Why don't you try it. You may find you like it. Some days it can be *very* stimulating."

Gaillac stepped back. Kinski found himself facing four groups of very frightened country folk. He unslung his rifle. His heart began to slam-dance in his chest. He couldn't just butcher these people. They stared at him like small, frightened animals. "Hmm" was all he said.

"What is it?" Gaillac asked.

"You know, I've been thinking," Kinski muttered, "if your boss—Robespierre?—meant what he said about an invasion and leaving you and me behind, I'd rather be dealing with a country that feared us than half a country who *hated* me and wanted to cut my throat."

Gaillac blinked in a bovine manner. "I don't understand."

"If we kill these two groups of people," Kinski said, "then these two groups will surely long for the day when they can get their hands on us. How many groups do you think there are right now, spread across this country?"

"I don't know," Gaillac said, attempting to calculate. "Thousands? Lots, anyhow."

"And what better time for them to get to us than while most of the military is over fighting in England?"

Gaillac frowned. "You're right. Let's kill them *all*."

He raised his gun. Kinski caught it by the muzzle. "Jean, you are a valiant warrior," Kinski said, nearly choking on the words, "but for a moment, try thinking like an explorer. You're wandering into territory you've never seen before. Suddenly a group of tribesmen appears out of nowhere. You kill half of them. The other half track you down and eventually kill you.

"But if, instead of killing the tribesmen, you *frighten* them, they won't come near you again. And if you ever come across them in the future, they'll be so afraid of you, you won't come to any harm."

Gaillac was blinking quickly now, looking like a walking semaphore code.

Kinski continued. "So what I propose we do is this: Instead of killing the citizens of this village, let's destroy the village. We'll leave the farmland, of course, since that's what the FSE is interested in, but let's smash up the town square, the homes, the businesses. Make the villagers fearful. This is what we are capable of. This and *more*, should they ever think of betraying the FSE. During the next four weeks let's try to frighten the people out of any thoughts of revolution."

Jean pondered Kinski's spiel for a full minute. "You know, Petrovich, that is a good idea. You must have been a good soldier. You may have just saved my life—in the future, I mean."

"My pleasure," Kinski said, his heart still pounding.

He watched silently as Gaillac signaled six of his men to round up all the villagers and place them at the far end of the main street, under guard.

Gaillac's Goons seemed confused at this last-minute change of agenda.

Jean then signaled his other men to march into the town

square. "Today, men, we are going to try something different. Instead of killing *people*, we will kill the town, eh? That will be fun!"

The young Goons shuffled about, kicking the dirt before them. They were clearly disappointed. Kinski sighed. These guys had IQs equal to their belt sizes.

Gaillac noted his troops' hesitation and walked up to a storefront window. Raising his rifle, he let off a few rounds, which obliterated the window. The sound of breaking glass and gunfire stirred his men.

"See?" he told them. "It's easy. It's fun. Now go kill the town!"

"Kill the town!" the men cried, taking their weapons and firing like crazy. Glass shattered. Wood splintered. Plaster chipped. The Goon Squad members sprayed everything in their sight, reducing the facades of the structures to nothing more than rubble. They then marched into the homes and stores and began pulverizing the interiors.

The townspeople watched, stunned, from the far end of town. Their lives had been spared, they knew, but now they were witnessing an act of supreme madness.

Kinski breathed a sigh of relief, knowing that he had saved a few lives and would probably save quite a few more with the same rap. Bullet-strewn villages could be rebuilt and repaired. Bullet-strewn hearts could not.

He became aware of the titanic form of Jean Gaillac towering at his right side. In one of Gaillac's paws was a frightened young girl, no more than fifteen years old.

"Here," Gaillac said, "have yourself your first French woman."

Gaillac thrust the girl at Kinski. Kinski pulled her, backward, to his chest. "Well, I . . ."

"Go ahead," Gaillac said, fondling the girl's chest. "She has nice titties. Take as long as you want. You can use the church. It's empty."

"Make love in a church?" Kinski gulped.

"No." Gaillac laughed. "Rape her in the church."

He snatched the gun from Kinski's hand and pushed Kinski and the struggling girl toward the oak doors leading to the town's only church.

Behind him, Gaillac's Goons continued murdering the village, their guns blazing.

Kinski continued to march up the steps, dragging the screaming girl beside him. Hell of a world, he thought to himself, hell of a world.

TWELVE

Kinski dragged the girl into the empty church. The thin young woman struggled and squirmed in his grasp. He was tired, frightened, and alone.

He was losing it.

He tossed the girl onto the marble floor of the tiny church. She landed on her back, legs spreadeagled. She wore a lightweight peasant skirt and a fluffy white blouse. Her straw-colored hair was tied behind her head in a ponytail.

In a minute Kinski was upon her, spreading his legs across her waist and pinning her hands down to the floor with his.

"Listen," he said in perfect French, "I am not who you think I am."

The girl cocked her head and stared at him. "You are scum."

"Maybe"—Kinski smiled—"but if I am, I'm my *own* kind of scum, not the FSE's."

"You are a killer, a rapist, a thief!" the girl declared.

Kinski sighed and stared into her frightened violet eyes. "Look, kid, I'm not going to hurt you. You're pretty. You're swell. But you're a little young for me, okay? And besides, I'm not in the habit of forcing myself on anyone. If a woman wants me, she comes and gets me."

"In your dreams," the girl said with a snarl.

"Maybe you're right, there," Kinski said, releasing her hands. He eased himself into a sitting position between her legs and produced a purloined comb. He passed the comb through his blond hair. "It *has* been a while. But duty comes first."

"Who are you? *What* are you?" the girl asked, raising her torso toward his.

"Who I am doesn't matter. What I am is a friend."

"I don't believe you."

Kinski sighed. "Listen, I could be signing my death warrant here, but I'm going to trust you. It seems to me that you are not enamored of the FSE."

"I have nothing to say."

"But you may be a supporter of Free France."

"I have never heard of them," the freckle-faced girl said, twisting her lips into a pout.

"Oh, Christ," Kinski said. "You're acting just like a woman. How old are you?"

"Fifteen."

"You've learned fast. I'm going to tell you something now. I'm going to let you in on a secret, a very big secret. But before I tell you, I want you to promise you won't turn me in."

"I promise nothing."

"Okay," Kinski said, replacing his comb, "let me rephrase that. If I hear that you've told anyone involved with the FSE what I'm about to explain, I'll hunt you down and kill you. I *will* have fun with you, and I *will* slit your throat afterward. Does that make you feel better?"

"This I understand, bastard," the girl said.

"What's your name?"

"Michelle."

"Okay, Michelle, here's the deal. I'm not with the FSE. They think I am but I'm not. Ever hear of the Marauders?"

"But of course," Michelle answered. "Everyone has heard of them. They are freedom fighters."

Kinski grinned impishly. "You're looking at one of them."

"I do not believe it."

"Doesn't matter to me if you do or not. The bottom line is: I'm stuck here. All alone. I was supposed to hook up with the Free Frenchies in Normandy. Something went wrong. I had to convince the FSE that I was for hire. Do you follow me?"

"Perhaps."

"You go to Catholic school?"

"Yes."

"That explains your attitude. Nuns, I bet."

"Dominican."

"The worst." Kinski grinned. "So what I'm going to do is try to get some of these Goon Squads to lay off your people. Have them shoot up the villages instead. Most of the leaders are dumb enough to do whatever I say, and as for their men . . ."

"They are dumber."

"Now you're catching on, kid." Kinski laughed. "I'll do what I can, but you and your people are going to have to do your part as well."

The girl stared at him sullenly. Kinski continued grinning. Damned if she wasn't cute.

He shook the thought from his mind. "Anyone you know who supports the Free French? Send them south, southwest, and southeast. Have them make contact with any freedom fighters they know of, have heard of. Within a month France may fall into the grasp of the FSE forever."

"England and America will help us," Michelle declared.

"Listen to me, kid, I don't have a lot of time here. Just listen and do what I tell you, okay? Within weeks the FSE will have thousands of soldiers in Paris. They're going to attack the United Kingdom and try to beat them back into the fold. If that happens, your Free France is dead. You got that?"

The girl nodded, stunned.

"Spread the word. Tell the Free French to be as aggressive as possible. And if they can, send any and all spare men and weaponry to Paris within the week. Have them settle outside the city limits. If and when things start to go 'pop,' tell them it's do-or-die time."

"Why do you trust me?" Michelle said.

Kinski shrugged. "I guess it's the hate in your eyes," he said, slowly getting to his feet. "Anyone who hates the Goon Squads that much can't be an FSE fan."

The girl smiled for the first time.

"Now," he said, extending a hand, "I want you to get up, tear up your blouse a bit, and take off your panties."

"What?"

"When you're done with that, start screaming bloody murder for about two minutes. I'll toss a few statues and votive candles around and yell a bit myself."

"That's sacrilege."

"No," Kinski corrected, "that's *smarts*. If I don't 'rape' you my way, you can bet that King Kong out there will do a great job of it his way. Your choice, kid."

Michelle sighed and slipped her panties down from beneath her flowing skirt. She grabbed her blouse and tore it in a single, downward, violent jerk.

"Great," Kinski said. "Toss the undies here."

Embarrassed, the girl did as she was told.

"Now yell your butt off," Kinski said, moving to the side of the church.

Michelle began screeching. The screams echoed and were amplified by the high, curved ceiling of the deserted church.

Kinski trotted to the side of the church and ripped a few wooden Station's of the Cross figurines out of the wall, tossing them violently against the wooden pews.

Crash.

"You bitch!" he bellowed in English.

Michelle screamed.

"You whore!" he yelled again, also in English.

He picked up a metal tray of votive candles and lifted it high into the air. Then he let it drop solidly onto the floor.

Keeee-rash.

"Take it. Take it!" he howled.

Michelle continued screeching.

Kinski padded up to her. "Okay, kid, I think that's enough. Let's give ourselves a minute or so of silence. This is the part where you swoon and I have a cigarette. Only you're not swooning and cigarettes are bad for your lungs."

The two stood together in the center of the church, waiting expectantly.

Kinski could sense the tension outside.

"Okay, good enough," Kinski said.

"You think so?" Michelle smiled.

"You're a good liar, almost as good as me. Now," he continued, pulling a .45, "I'm going to fire this gun. The noise will be louder because we're in an abandoned building. Do you have a fingernail-clipper or something sharp?"

"No."

He pulled out an old-fashioned dirk. "Here, be careful with it. Prick your finger."

"Why?"

"Prick your finger, not a lot, and spread the blood on your underwear here."

He ripped her panties nearly in two and handed them back to her. The girl, sensing the direction he was heading, did as she was told. She winced as the tip of the knife sliced her thumb. Several droplets of blood bubbled forth. She quickly wiped them on her panties.

"Now, for best results," Kinski said, "swing your arm around and around ten times."

Michelle did just that. On the count of eleven she lowered her arm. Her thumb was drenched in blood.

"Don't be afraid," Kinski said. "That's what was supposed to happen. Now wipe the blood on your underwear."

Michelle grasped her thumb with her torn panties. Before long, half of the underwear was dotted with blood.

"Okay," Kinski said, grabbing the panties. "I'm going to fire the gun, you're going to scream one last time, and then you're going to go into the back of the church and hide until you hear us leave."

"What you said before," Michelle said. "It was all true?"

"I lie to a lot of people, kid," Kinski said with a smile, "but never to someone I have to depend on."

"You are one of the Marauders?"

"I am."

She threw her arms around him and kissed him on the mouth.

Kinski's head spun momentarily. He broke her embrace. "Thanks. Now cover your ears."

Michelle clasped her hands over her ears.

Kinski raised his .45 and fired a single round into the church's ceiling.

Michelle opened her mouth and shrieked, hamming it up a bit, allowing the shriek to dribble off into a moan.

"You have a career ahead of you in the theater," Kinski said. "Now remember, trust only those you know to be Free French."

"I will, Monsieur Marauder." She smiled. "Thank you for my life."

"No problem," Kinski said. "Before you go, wait a minute . . ."

He fished into his pocket and pulled out a handful of

francs. "Take these. When you're eighteen, give me a call in England. You can reach me at the palace. Just say you're a distant relative of Kinski's."

"I will do just that."

"I'm counting on it," Kinski said. "Now get the hell out of here."

He watched the young girl trot down the center aisle and exit the church through the sacristy on the left of the altar.

He smiled to himself. He might get himself out of this mess eventually, if he could stall the Goon Squad long enough.

He waited a few seconds before unslinging his AK-47.

He placed the pair of bloodied panties on the muzzle of his gun.

He headed for the door. Reaching it, he kicked it open violently with his left foot.

He slowly walked down the front steps of the church.

He felt the angry stares of the villagers slice into his body. They'd understand eventually, he surmised.

He affixed a callous smile to his face. The FSE troops were grouped directly in front of the church steps.

He continued to march forward.

He saw the bearlike Gaillac lumber forward. "You had a good time, eh, my friend?"

"A very good time," Kinski said with a sneer, trying to out-Clint-Eastwood Clint Eastwood (thank God he spent his childhood watching reruns of old spaghetti Westerns).

"I could use a cigarette," Kinski said in a monotone.

Jean Gaillac produced one. He placed it between Kinski's chapped lips. "I'll light you."

"Thanks."

The cigarette flared under the fire produced by an ancient lighter. Kinski puffed on it. He never had learned how to take a deep drag. By the time he was a teenager, it was almost against the law to smoke a cigarette.

"Here," he said, tossing the panties to Jean. "I brought you a souvenir."

Jean's pockmarked face twisted itself into the fleshy equivalent of an exclamation point. "Even in there you thought of me?"

"You're the boss." Kinski shrugged. "You're the one who gave me the gift."

"And the gift?"

"She won't be given to another?"

"You find French women . . . *amusing*?"

"Very much so."

Jean Gaillac tossed the bloodied panties onto the ground and leapt forward, embracing the sinewy Kinski in a bear hold. "*Mon frère . . . My brother . . .* you are the kindred spirit I have been looking for all my life."

Kinski's eyes bulged, bullfrog-style, in the massive embrace of Gaillac.

"The feeling's mutual," he said, wheezing.

Gaillac lowered Kinski to the ground. "Petrovich, I sense we will do great things together, more than anyone could ever dream of. Imagine how surprised that weasel Robespierre will be!"

"That's the only thing that's keeping me going." Kinski coughed.

"Come," Jean Gaillac said, wrapping a tendrillike arm around Kinski's thin neck. "We have other assignments before us. We will exceed the FSE's wildest dreams."

"Be still, my heart," Kinski said, trying to will some fresh air into his battered, tattered lungs.

THIRTEEN

Crazy Jack Keenan watched as the last of the military armaments were loaded on a rustic wagon. "That looks good," he said, nodding.

Marie waddled up alongside him. "Now, do we merely wheel our arms along the Seine?"

"No," Jack said thoughtfully, "you cover each truck with pitchforksful of hay."

"Buddha Chan sidled up to Jack. "Will that be enough?"

"Probably not, but it's all we have going for us for the time being," he said.

He glanced at the small road, winding along the bank of the Seine. "Who'd attack farm folk, right?"

"The FSE?" Buddha Chan asked.

"If they do, we'll take them out. That's the end of the discussion," Jack stated.

Mamudi ran up to the trio, obviously ogling Marie with his one good eye. "I've rigged the mines, Jack."

"I knew you could."

"Should I put them in the river now?"

"No," Jack replied. "Let's wait until we really need them. I mean, how many FSE troops can be around here? Our intelligence shows that the FSE is fragmented in France. All we have to do is hump it up the river, enter Paris, and take the Goons out. It shouldn't be too much of a problem."

Mamudi grinned, creasing his scar. "I love easy jobs. It makes me feel so spiritual."

Jack tried to ignore him. "I bet it does. Marie, I have a big favor to ask from your supporters. On the way to the first outpost, I want half of them slogging through the water at the river's edge, divided into two companies, one on each side of the Seine. I want them alert and armed. I want them to shoot at *any*thing that doesn't look right."

"That can be done."

"We'll proceed with the caravan on the north side of the Seine, since that's where most of the outposts are."

Marie crossed her bulky arms. "Agreed."

"I'll walk point," Buddha Chan said, adjusting his gold shooter's glasses.

"Fine," Jack said.

"And I," Mamudi announced, "will be Mademoiselle Marrette's personal bodyguard."

Jack scratched his matted orange hair with a dirt-encrusted hand. "Now how did I know that was coming?"

"You are a true mystic warrior." Mamudi grinned. "Perhaps, long ago, you would have been a world leader."

"I have trouble going to the grocery store in this damn world," Jack grunted. "Now get Marie the hell outa here."

Crazy Jack Keenan watched his fellow Marauders and their newfound compatriots prepare the march toward Paris. He felt his facial muscles sag. He'd feel a lot better if he knew for sure that King Shatterhand realized three of the four Marauders had not only made it ashore, but also had made contact with Free France and were now planning their first major upset.

He frowned, thinking of Kinski. He'd feel better if he knew that Kinski hadn't survived the attack, wasn't a prisoner in some podunk village, held captive by some imbecilic farm boy in an FSE tunic.

Jack shook the thoughts from his head.

He had only one way to go.

Forward.

In London, in Hyde Park, hundreds of thousands of British citizens turned out to pay their respects to the late great Marauders.

King Shatterhand spoke before the four symbolic graves, placed in a newly constructed gazebo not far from Speakers' Corner, a place where, before the war, and now, for the first time afterward, anyone could grab a soapbox, stand on it, and speak his or her mind about anything.

"Fellow patriots," the king announced. "I am here to officially announce that our quartet of American freedom fighters, the Marauders, have perished while trying to contact the French underground."

The citizenry, which had either read the news in the previous day's papers or watched it on the newly revived BBC stations, uttered mournful sounds.

"The FSE has robbed us of four of our staunchest allies . . . four men who could do the work of a thousand times their number. So today I will not mourn them. I will *celebrate* them."

The crowd murmured.

"Today we have but one goal. To avenge their deaths," Shatterhand intoned.

The crowd began to rally.

"To all in the armed forces, I urge you to increase learning your skills!"

The crowd began to applaud.

"To all those in the civilian populace, I urge you to increase your output of goods and services!"

The crowd cheered.

"To all those within hearing distance, I urge you to increase your determination! Within six months I want to see United Kingdom troops storming the beaches of Normandy fully trained and well armed. I want to see the FSE beaten back from France. I want to see France join the rebellion! I want to see the ones left in Great Britain continue to work and toil to make our New World a stable and just society in which to live."

He paused as the ever-growing crowd grew wild with cheering and huzzahs.

"And most of all," Shatterhand concluded, "I want this day, June tenth, ever to be remembered and respected as the Day of the Marauders."

The crowd erupted into an elephantine cheer.

Shatterhand faced his subjects. "We *will* win. It is our *destiny* to win."

He walked away from the microphone on the podium. A dozen Scots guards, clad in kilts, began playing "Amazing Grace" on their bagpipes. The crowd lapsed into silence.

The eerie wail of the pipes caressed the vast grounds of

Kensington Gardens, now teeming with Britishers.

The only sound louder than the pipers were those of the snifflers on hand.

Finally the age-old hymn ceased.

A group of Royal Guardsman strode forward, rifles clutched before their chests.

They stood at attention over the four mock graves.

They aimed their rifles toward the bright sky.

A twenty-one-gun salute commenced. *Crackity-crack-crack-crack.*

The crowd gasped collectively.

The last burst finally echoed through the sky.

The crowd stood before the mock graves, stunned.

Shatterhand calmly walked up to the microphone. "Revenge!" he cried.

"Revenge," the crowd echoed.

"Freedom!" he bellowed.

"Freedom!" the crowd responded.

"Courage in all we do!" he cried, raising a leather-encased gnarled fist heavenward.

"Courage!" the crowd screamed.

King Shatterhand smiled at them. He slowly backed away from the podium and turned to an aide named McGuire. "Let's get the hell out of here," he said with a sigh. "I feel like I'm either going to pass out or kill myself."

The young aide shunted the king to the side of the podium.

Shatterhand sighed. "Actually, I'd settle for puking on my shoes."

"Things can't be as bad as that, Your Highness. Easy down the steps, sir."

"Things are worse, son. I've lost four good friends and the only hope I've ever had."

Shatterhand's aide swallowed hard. He had never seen the king so depressed. He felt sad. He felt like pissing down his pants in fright.

Shatterhand strode toward the awaiting limousine. "I want the radiomen to increase their efforts to contact Free France."

"Yes, sir."

"I want any and all activities along the western shore of France to be monitored."

"Yes, sir."

"Contact our Interpol friends. If they hear of anything out of the ordinary, I want them to spill their guts."

"We haven't been able to raise them in days, sir."

"That's not a good sign. What shape is the RAF in?"

"A dozen planes in service, two dozen being rebuilt."

"Damn," Shatterhand muttered. "So we can't risk any reconnaissance flights."

"I don't think so, sir. In another few months, perhaps."

"We don't have that kind of time."

"Yes, sir."

The aide flung open the left rear door of the limousine and Shatterhand lowered his titanic body into the car.

"I wish there was something we could do *now*."

"I'm afraid there isn't, sir."

"Thank you for reminding me of that," Shatterhand muttered.

His aide slammed the door shut and the limousine sped off, back toward the palace.

Thousands of sniffling, crying citizens remained in Hyde Park in the wake of the speeding limo.

FOURTEEN

Gaillac aimed his jeep at a farmhouse near Nemours. "This should prove amusing," the shaggy-headed giant said.

Kinski, uncomfortable in the passenger's seat, frowned. "How so?"

"The people on this farm? They are known collaborators with Free France. A few days ago we blew up a radio transmitter, the one that the Resistance was using to contact England. Two of the men on the farm were seen running away from the site. They were the only ones who survived. That night we cut down the pigs who weren't blown up.

"So now we go to visit the home of the traitors. What we have to do is torture them for information. I've always enjoyed torture. How about you?"

"I've never tried it," Kinski muttered.

"You should. It can be fun . . . especially if the victim is a *très jolie jeune fille*, a very pretty young girl."

"I'll try to remember that."

"You seem disturbed."

Kinski heaved a massive sigh. "I just think the FSE is going about this all wrong."

"What do you mean?"

"I mean this: You torture a few people, maybe you get the information. Maybe. If you do or if you don't, you kill the people, anyway. By now everyone in this country knows your methods. It doesn't matter to them if they talk or not, they know they're going to experience a lot of pain and, no matter what, be killed."

"That is good, no?" Jean asked.

"No," Kinski repeated. "It's not."

Jean sighed. "I don't understand you . . . *again*."

Kinski suppressed a smile that was daring to creep across his face. "Don't you understand? These people know that once the Goon Squads show up, they're dead—no matter what they do. Why should they voluntarily give you any information about Free France? They're already doomed to die."

Jean nodded, angling his jeep toward an upgrade in the road. "I have never thought about it that way."

"The FSE has a lot to learn from the Russian KGB," Kinski muttered.

"KGB? You were part of the KGB?"

Kinski offered a sly grin. "Not officially," he said. "But I've heard of their methods. In fact, rumor has it that before the war, they had Russian KGB spies in all of the Eastern Bloc countries. Surveillance, mostly . . . it's rumored."

"About these KGB methods you heard about . . . ?"

"For instance, the KGB, if they really wanted information from a prisoner, wouldn't just bully him or torture him. They'd arrange for him to think for himself, make his own decision. They'd give him the option to cooperate."

"How?"

"Okay," Kinski said, his mind spiraling into high gear. "Here's the setup we'd use if we were KGB. You storm into a place, arrest your prisoners, rough them up a little, badger them a lot. They don't like you. They're waiting to die. Just before you're obviously going to kill them, I walk in."

"And?"

"And I order you out of the room."

"How could you do that?"

"It's a game, Jean. I order you out of the room for acting like a Goon, okay? Then I quietly sit with the people and talk things out with them. Tell them that I'm sorry, you shouldn't have gone that far. I empathize with their position, but in turn, they should realize mine. I am a soldier of the FSE. I need information. I don't want to hurt them or anybody else. If they cooperate and give me the information we need, they can go.

"Then I swear to them that all those they betray will not be murdered. They will, instead, be imprisoned and treated fairly. So they relax. They spill their guts. We go away with information, and we didn't have to waste a lot of time torturing our victims."

"But you don't speak French," Jean stated.

"Most people in this country can speak a smattering of English, right?"

"Yes, but begrudgingly."

"If their lives depended upon it?"

"They'd talk," Jean admitted.

"So there you go," Kinski replied.

"What happens to the people after they 'spill their guts'?" Jean asked.

"We waste them." Kinski smiled. "Or rather, *I* waste them. Preferably not in their home. I take them to a secluded area, maybe the woods. They trust me. They think they're going to go free. They trust me, you see. That's a very important point to remember.

"I let them dash forward for a few yards, and then I raise my gun. *Wham!* It's all over."

"Magnificent," Jean said enthusiastically. "I bet we could blame their deaths on Free France. Imagine what the people would think of the Free French executing ordinary people because they didn't support the insurrectionist movement."

"Now you're catching on," Kinski said. If Jean were any dumber, he'd be a beet.

"Do you *really* think such a tactic will work?"

"There's only one way to find out." Kinski shrugged.

"We should be arriving at the farm in five minutes." Jean chortled. "*Then* we will find out."

Kinski nodded silently. He leaned back in the jeep and closed his eyes. He had a pounding headache. He was in the middle of a war-torn country, one side ready to tear out the belly of the other. Plus, one side was planning on obliterating his new homeland, the United Kingdom.

As far as he knew, Crazy Jack, Buddha Chan, and Freddie were dead.

There was no one to stop the FSE from ruling Europe in toto.

Except, perhaps, for one poor slob named Peter Kinski.

Kinski frowned. He didn't like the idea of being a one-man guerrilla unit.

Suddenly he brightened. What the hell. A couple of days ago he hadn't liked being part of a four-man guerrilla squad. He hadn't known how easy he had had it then.

Kinski opened his eyes. The French countryside whizzed by him. He glanced over at Gaillac, inwardly seething. He would churn things up as much as he could. He owed it to Crazy Jack, Buddha Chan, and Freddie.

Gaillac turned toward him. "This is a good life, is it not?"

"Beats farming," Kinski answered.

"You and me"—Jean chuckled—"we are two of a kind."

"Yeah," Kinski muttered. "We're real heroes."

Gaillac emitted a braying laugh as he pushed down on the gas pedal.

Kinski continued to regard the man in silence. He knew only one thing: Whether he succeeded in thwarting the FSE attack on Britain or not, before he was captured, he'd kill Gaillac with his own hands.

Gaillac . . . the man who had slaughtered the Marauders.

FIFTEEN

Marius Valjean sat at the front window of his small farm-house, shotgun in hand.

His son, Philippe, paced in the kitchen behind him while his mother, Cosette, sat silently at the kitchen table.

Marius scanned the surrounding hillside for any sign of trouble.

"This is no good, Marius," Cosette said.

"Maybe they won't come," Philippe said.

"They saw us, son," Marius replied. "They'll come for us. They're bound to."

"And when they do?"

"We will die," Marius replied.

Cosette shuddered.

"So maybe it's best we kill each other," Philippe said with a smirk. "At least that way we will die with dignity."

"Suicide isn't dignified," Marius replied, his gaze drifting to the hog trough outside the barn. "I'd rather die at the hands of a two-legged snail than take the life of one I love."

Philippe nodded. "I wish we knew when they were going to arrive."

A bullet sailed through the front window, sending Marius to the ground and Philippe diving atop his mother, thrusting her down onto the kitchen floor.

"You've gotten your wish," Marius grunted as automatic fire sliced through the two-hundred-year-old home.

Marius covered his head as the walls around him began to fragment. Philippe began cursing, covering his mother with his own body.

"Don't swear, son," Cosette whispered.

"Fuck swearing!" Philippe spat back. "We're dead now."

The front door of the farmhouse burst in. Jean Gaillac stood in the portal—bearlike, ferocious. Marius made a move for his discarded shotgun. Jean kicked it away with a defiant laugh. "You won't be able to use that, old man."

Jean extended a massive hand and lifted the gray-haired elder up by his collar. "Look outside, traitor!"

Marius glanced to his left. Parked outside the house were two trucks.

Three dozen FSE Goons stood flanking the building, automatic weapons poised.

"Do you want to try to run for it?" Jean encouraged.

"I have nothing to run from," Marius wheezed.

Jean tossed the man back down on the ground. "Excellent. You and Sonny stand. Let Mama remain where she is, on the floor, like any good, subservient female."

Cosette looked up from the floor. "Eat dung and die."

Jean walked into the kitchen, dragging Marius behind him. He raised a boot to the elderly woman's face. "Would you like your head splattered on the floor, Grandmother?"

"I'm no relative of yours," Cosette stated.

"You're not good enough," Jean said, tossing Marius into a corner and dragging Philippe there as well.

Jean pulled out a Colt .45 pistol. "Now," he said, training the weapon on the two men, "let's chat."

Marius said nothing.

Neither did his son.

"I don't think you undrstand me," Jean continued. "I *know* you are part of Free France. You were identified at the Normandy Beach radio shack the other night. Positively identified."

"We are farmers," Marius said. "Nothing more."

Jean smiled. He swung the pistol, butt first, into the elderly man's face.

Marius groaned as the gun butt sliced a large hole under his left cheekbone. "Wrong answer," Jean said, seething.

"We don't know what you're talking about," Philippe said, taking his father into his arms.

"Right," Jean replied.

"Scum," Cosette muttered from the floor.

Jean swung his right arm around and fired a shot into the

kitchen's spice cupboard, sending three dozen small bottles of herbs and seasonings down on the woman's head. "Silence, Grandma," he whispered.

Cosette stared at him from the floor.

Jean smiled at her. "The next shot could be lower."

Gaillac turned to the two cowering men. "So what do I have to do to convince you I want answers, eh? Do I have to take out an eye? Slice off an ear? Would you like a finger or two blown off?"

"We know nothing," Marius said.

"Well," Jean said, raising his revolver, "then I suppose you die for nothing."

At that point Kinski burst into the kitchen. "Wait!" he cried in English. "What are you doing?"

Jean lapsed into a melodramatic silence before replying, "Obeying orders."

Kinski stared at the family. "I issue new orders."

He watched for a reaction. Only Philippe understood what he was saying. Good, Kinski thought, the boy understands English. He can translate.

"You've overstepped your bounds," Kinski said, raising his AK-47 in Gaillac's direction. "Out of here now, you Goon."

Jean attempted a sneer. In reality the expression resembled that of a bench-presser with a groin injury, but it was better than nothing.

Jean skittered out of the room.

Kinski waited until Jean was out of the house before he turned to the family. He focused on Philippe, speaking in fluent French. "You understood what I just said?"

Philippe nodded. "Yes . . . so?"

"Well, I'm not working with that man. I'm working with Free France."

The entire family regarded Kinski with incredulous looks.

Kinski shrugged. "Here's what we're going to do. I'm going to lead you out into the woods out back. I'm going to sit with you and explain what's going on and why it's important to rally whoever you know connected with Free France. After that you're on your own. Go to a friend's house. Go wherever you want to.

"Whatever you do, don't return to your home for at least a month. We can lock things up before we leave. You can contact your neighbors to provide for the livestock, but you can't return."

"What are you going to do to us?" Marius asked.

"Set you free," Kinski replied. "After we chat in the woods I'll shoot a few trees. I'll report that I've killed you. Everything will be all right."

"Why are you doing this?" Cosette asked. "You are not French."

"No," Kinski admitted. "I'm American."

"American?" Philippe exclaimed. "That's impossible! There have been no Americans here since the Last Great War."

"Except . . . ," Marius whispered.

Kinski nodded. "Yeah, except . . ."

"The Marauders?" Marius rejoined.

"I'm one of them," Kinski acknowledged. "Now, when you leave here, I want you to contact anybody and everybody in Free France you know. Try to reestablish radio contact with England. Get a message to Shatterhand that the Marauders' mission is on. Crazy Jack, Buddha Chan, and Freddie may be dead, but Kinski is alive and well and living up to his nickname. Shatterhand will know what you're talking about."

Kinski took a deep breath. "And if you can't do that, gather as many supporters as possible and have them gather, gradually, outside Paris within the next week."

"For what reason?" Marius asked.

"Very, very soon all hell is going to break loose. It could mean the end of your country. If you trust me, you'll be there to prevent it."

Marius nodded. "I trust you."

"Good," Kinski rejoined. "Now stash what you feel is valuable, lock up the house, and then, with you at gunpoint, we'll leave."

"For where?" Cosette asked.

"Into the woods." Kinski smiled. "And after that? Wherever you feel safest."

Outside the farmhouse, Jean Gaillac stood, smirking with his hayseed Goon Squad. "This man," he muttered to the man to his left, "he has brains. You watch what greatness we will achieve for the FSE."

The boy next to him, a lad of eighteen with an IQ to match, nodded dumbly.

Jean watched as Kinski led the three people out of the house at gunpoint. Kinski marched the trio into the nearby woods.

"We will take the resistance by cunning," Jean declared.

The boy next to him nodded idiotically.

Jean watched the threesome disappear into the woods. He lit a cigarette. It smelled like cabbage. He waited in silence. This was the part he wished he could have seen—Kinski leading the three innocents into the woods and then blowing them apart. Ah, sweet slaughter.

He stiffened as the familiar *crackity-crack* sound of an AK-47 echoed through the woods.

He took a deep drag from his cigarette.

Christ, it was good to be alive. Good to be working for a cause.

It didn't matter, exactly, if it was his or not.

A minute later Kinski emerged from the woods.

He walked up to Gaillac.

"What have you found out?" Gaillac asked.

Kinski grinned. Silver Tongue slid into action. "It's nothing you want to know about."

"I don't understand . . . *again*."

"Those Americans you killed the other night?"

"Yes?"

"It's possible you didn't kill them."

"What?"

"It's possible they were saved from death."

"Who? Who did such a thing?"

"FSE men."

"Are you sure?"

"That's the rumor they had heard. All I know is that there are Americans operating in France."

"Names! I need names!"

"Don't have them."

"Who could it be?"

"Someone very high up is collaborating with Free France, it seems."

"But there are no higher-ups in the FSE—"

"Except . . ."

Jean slapped himself on the side of his square head. "Except for Giles Robespierre!"

"I didn't say that." Kinski shrugged. "I need much more information before I draw any conclusions. After all, these are just rumors. However, most rumors have a basis in truth."

"My own boss . . . a traitor?"

"He may not be," Kinski cautioned.

"What should I do?" Jean implored.

"Examine each order he gives you," Kinski advised. "Evaluate it on your own. If it seems right, obey it. If it seems strange, avoid it. That's all I can say. After all, I'm a stranger here."

Jean wrapped a massive arm around Kinski's thin shoulders. "You are a good soldier, my friend. An excellent comrade. I will trust your judgment."

"If that's what you want . . ."

"That's what I depend on. No doubt I will be getting many conflicting orders in the weeks ahead. If Giles is a traitor, he will have us running around the entire country chasing our tails."

"So?"

"I will trust you to decipher the orders. Let me know which are real and which are not."

"I am not a Frenchman. I can only guess."

"You are a soldier. You will *know*."

Kinski felt a smile forming. "And what about Robespierre?"

"Let him rot in hell!" Jean declared.

"That has a nice ring to it," Kinski said. "What now?"

"Let's get the hell out of here and on to our next assignment," Jean muttered.

"Okay," Kinski replied. He watched the angry giant lumber toward his jeep.

He was shaken. He was defeated. It was Kinski's game now.

Kinski vowed to make him pay.

Pay for murdering Kinski's three closest friends in the world.

Kinski sighed and glanced at the countryside around him.

He had many more lies to tell, many more stories to fabricate. He hoped he could keep track of them all.

Lies had a way of taking on a life of their own. And when the lies took over, that's when the liar found himself up against it in a big way.

SIXTEEN

Under the shroud of darkness the Marauders' caravan edged slowly up the Seine. Mamudi rode with Marie in the first of six wagons stacked with hay. Crazy Jack preferred to walk. Buddha Chan was up in front of the caravan, walking point.

In the river below them, on both sides of the bank, four dozen soggy revolutionaries slogged, fighting off both drowsiness and mosquitoes.

"I wish you wouldn't lean so close to me," Marie said to Mamudi.

"I am your bodyguard," said Mamudi, shifting the hay wagon's gears. "I'm only doing what is expected of me."

Marie sighed. "How did you lose your eye?"

"Afghanistan," Mamudi said with a shrug. "A Russian sniper. He was quick, I was slow. It happens."

"You don't mind it?"

"Mademoiselle," Freddie said, smiling, "I am a Sunni Muslim. You accept what is given to you. You try your best to change what is bad, in store, for others. That is my credo. That is why I still fight. My faith dictates it."

"You're awfully thin for a soldier."

"I have inner strengths," Mamudi said, steering the caravan forward. "I would love to share them with you."

"I bet," Marie muttered.

Mamudi hit the brakes. From a hundred feet ahead, Jack was signaling to stop.

A rotund figure jogged into the picture.

"Excuse me, my dear," Mamudi said, bolting out of the cab of the truck.

He jogged forward to join Crazy Jack. Buddha Chan trotted up to both men. "We have a problem," he said.

Jack sighed. "Now how did I know this was coming?"

"There's an FSE contingent two miles down the road."

"So?"

"It's not what we expected."

Mamudi squinted at Buddah Chan. "In what way?"

"These guys are heavily armed. Trained military men. They're not farm boys, that's for sure."

"Heavily armed?" Jack asked.

"And then some," Chan replied.

"Shit," Jack hissed. "I knew this was too good a plan."

Marie waddled up to the trio. "What's up?"

"Nothing you should concern yourself about, *chérie*," Mamudi said with a formal bow.

"Can it, Muslim," Marie said. "What's wrong?"

Jack grimaced. "Our intelligence is apparently wrong about the strength of the FSE in these parts. There's a mini-army of FSE Goons blocking our path. They're not local jerks, either. Apparently the FSE is getting frisky in France."

"So," Marie asked, "now what?"

Buddha Chan rubbed his itchy, bald scalp. "The three of us go ahead and try to take them out."

"You mean the *four* of us," Marie replied.

"No," Jack stated. "The *three* of us. We are trained soldiers, Marie. We know how to deal with combat. You are a brave, heroic rebel, but when push comes to shove, you'd be eliminated in a second if these guys are real pros. You're more valuable alive and leading your people than getting wasted in an ambush."

"You think so?" Marie said, pushing her massive body against that of Jack. "You think I can't handle myself?"

"These people are killers," Jack said, finding himself being knocked back two feet by the woman's sheer size.

"Those people know of no cause. They are mercenaries. They have no passion."

Mamudi wedged his angular body between the two giants.

"Marie," he cautioned, "remember, we want victory, not needless slaughter."

Marie eyeballed Mamudi. "Don't treat me like a *woman*."

"Ah," Mamudi said, "but that is impossible. You are a *glorious* woman. Delicious. You are also a fighter, but a local one. My friends and I have seen many things. It would be better if you remained here with your troops. Allow us to go forward and check out the enemy. If anything happens to us, well, you'll still be here to lead the charge forward. Militarily, strategically, that makes sense, doesn't it?"

Marie grinned. "I suppose so. You have a way with words, you know that?"

Mamudi took the liberty of tickling her double chin. "Yes, but I am selfish too. I don't want anything to happen to my next wife."

Marie sighed. "Freddie . . . don't act like an ass."

Mamudi winked at her. "If true love makes me resemble an ass, I accept the role gladly."

Marie trained her gaze on Buddha Chan and Crazy Jack. "What should I do?"

"Keep your men here until you hear from us," Jack said.

"If we're not back in four hours," Buddha Chan began, "prepare your troops for all-out warfare. Take out the FSE Goons and proceed toward Paris as planned."

Marie nodded. The three Marauders faced each other.

"This will be interesting," Buddha Chan stated.

Crazy Jack slapped his hand against his AK-47. "This could be suicide."

Mamudi shrugged, raising his AK-47 and patting his knives that were safely sheathed in his combat belt.

"This is what we're here for," he said.

"Let's go," Jack uttered.

"I'll lead the way," Buddha Chan said, his corpulent form jogging into the night mist.

"I'll see you again," Mamudi called over his shoulder to Marie.

Marie waited for the three men to disappear before she picked up an M16 and waddled forward. "Sooner than you think, lover boy."

Marie marched forward.

Several of her men trotted behind her. She spun around and faced them. "You stay put," she ordered. "We have trouble up ahead. If I'm not back in three hours, get going and get tough. We're being watched. We're being lured into an ambush. So get the lead out, kids. It's time to do or die!"

SEVENTEEN

The three Marauders jogged forward under the misty night sky.

"They're up ahead," Buddha Chan said, "to the left of the road."

"How many?" Crazy Jack snapped.

"Couldn't tell," Buddha Chan replied. "At least three dozen or more. Very, very armed."

Mamudi stiffened. "Point men. Two of them."

"Shit," Crazy Jack hissed. The trio backed into the foliage. "You know the drill," he added.

Mamudi stayed behind.

Crazy Jack and Buddha Chan continued to run forward in the underbrush. Mamudi positioned himself in the shrubbery, lurking, ready to ambush. He unsheathed his British-issue Fairbairn-Sykes Commando knife. He waited.

Up ahead, Buddha Chan and Crazy Jack awaited their prey. The first point men walked by them. They didn't move. "Your call," Jack whispered.

"I'll take him," Buddha Chan said with a grimace.

Buddha Chan knew that the second point man would be trailing the first by approximately fifty meters. He took in a deep breath of damp night air. There was no room for failure.

He *sensed* the footsteps before he actually heard them: combat boots on frost-covered grass.

The second point man strolled by them, his automatic rifle trained on the land before him.

Buddha Chan leapt into action. He padded behind the man, amazingly agile and quick for someone of his size. He jerked the startled point man's head back by pushing his index and middle fingers into the soldier's nostrils.

The point man's throat was exposed. He attempted to cry out, but Buddha Chan refused him the chance. The enemy soldier's eyes widened as the blur that was Chan engulfed him. Buddha raised his knife and then drove it through the Goon's throat from the right to the left. He then slashed outward, nearly decapitating his victim. The entire move took less than an instant.

When the point man sagged, Buddha Chan quickly pulled the body off the trail.

No one in the main force, behind the point man, would notice a thing.

Meanwhile, up front, a hundred meters in front of Buddha Chan, Mamudi executed a similar action on the first point man.

The skinny, one-eyed soldier nearly had to leap on the burly FSE man's back. The Goon was a good six inches taller than Freddie. Mamudi grunted as he yanked back the bull-necked guard's head.

"Killer of the innocent," he eulogized, plunging the knife into the smooth neck.

When he was done, he lugged the burly body into the underbrush and trotted along the path, rejoining his two comrades.

"I don't like this at all," Crazy Jack said.

"Yeah." Buddha Chan nodded. "My guy was about as French as I am."

"Mine too," Mamudi concurred.

"Definitely Eastern European," Buddha Chan said with a sigh. "Looks like we've stepped in it up to our noses this time. What the hell is an invastion force doing out here in the boonies?"

"Let's slog forward," Jack said, raising his AK-47, "and find out. Get ready to rock and roll."

Buddha Chan raised his trusty M16. "Well, at least this time we're the ones calling the shots," he said.

"I hope," Jack whispered.

Mamudi raised his AK-47. "Let's see what kind of fighting men we're up against."

The trio jogged forward into the darkness. Behind them, in

the thick underbrush, a massive figure plowed through the forest. It was Marie Marrette . . . and she had a score to settle.

She paused behind the body of the first point man, gazing passively at his face, caught for all eternity in a mask of both shock and horror.

"Goddamn foreigner," she said, giving the body a sharp kick in the abdomen.

She rumbled through the woods a few meters more and encountered the second felled FSE Goon.

This time she planted a titanic foot on the cadaver's stomach and pressed down hard.

Blood gushed from the man's already savaged neck.

"Rot in hell," she said, seething.

She grasped her rifle and, worked up into a simmering desire for blood, plowed through the forest, knocking down any shrubbery in her path.

EIGHTEEN

The three Marauders scurried through the damp underbrush, Buddha Chan in the lead.

"There," he said, pointing, "up ahead."

"Christ," Crazy Jack hissed. "Look at those guys."

"On the plus side," Mamudi theorized, "they're bunking down for the night."

"Now why doesn't that make me feel any better?" Crazy Jack muttered.

In the wilderness ahead, three dozen highly trained FSE men set up camp for the night.

There were two truckloads of them.

Plus a jeep.

The jeep boasted a 60-mm machine gun.

There were also 60-mm mortars present.

As well as a few Soviet/ChiCom RPG-2 rocket launchers, commonly called B-40s in Southeast Asia. Those weapons were smoothbore, muzzle-loaded, shoulder-fired, recoilless beauties that fired a 40-mm spin-stabilized round. It weighed but 6.3 pounds, was 3.2 feet in length, and had a muzzle velocity of 84 meters per second with an effective range of 100 meters.

"Looks like they know we're here," Crazy Jack muttered.

"Looks like our information was incorrect," Buddha Chan acknowledged. "These boys are professionals."

"Those boys are definitely from Eastern Europe," Mamudi replied. "Polskies, Czechs, Russkies. Not a Frenchman among them. Probably part of Maximov's elite guard . . . the ones who have been kicking the bejeebers out of the Eastern Bloc countries since the last war."

"So what are they up to?" Crazy Jack asked.

"I don't want to think about it," Mamudi replied.

"We have to take them out," Buddha Chan said.

"Okay," Crazy Jack said. "I want you two to fan out."

"Open fire?"

"Not until you see me run toward the jeep. I have to get my hands on the machine gun," Crazy Jack stated.

"Jack," Buddha Chan said, "that's not the smartest move in the world. You know that."

Jack shrugged. "Smart, no. Practical, yes. If we go slamming in there and they open up on us with that baby, we'll be looking like roadkill in a matter of seconds."

"We have to get them caught up in a crossfire," Mamudi declared. "They won't know where we're zapping them from."

"No problem," Buddha Chan replied.

"Just keep shifting positions," Jack cautioned. "I need them to be caught *totally* off-guard."

"Shoot to kill?" Mamudi asked.

"Natch," Crazy Jack said. "But if you can, try to cripple. We need information—desperately."

Jack rubbed his bushy head of flame-red hair. "We're stuck here, guys. We can't contact Shatterhand. We don't know *what* we're up against. We have a lot of questions to ask. Dead men don't answer questions."

"I hear you," Buddha Chan stated.

"So," Mamudi said, taking a deep breath of dank night air, "shall we rock and roll?"

"Definitely," Buddha Chan replied.

Jack turned to his two comrades. "Hey, if anything goes wrong . . . I'll see you in hell."

Buddha Chan nodded. "Again?"

Mamudi smiled. "Only if we have bunk beds in our barracks."

"Bad angels deserve at least *that* much," Crazy Jack replied, slithering out of sight.

He kept low to the ground, sometimes scrambling down toward the assembled troops on all fours.

The men below him conversed in a language he didn't recognize.

Sure as hell, it wasn't French.

Crazy Jack peered down into the camp. Damn. Leaning against the jeep was a radioman, chatting up a storm.

When the attack came, he'd have to squelch the radio first off. Big priority. Jack didn't know how many troops were in the area. He didn't want to run the risk of taking out this bunch, only to have the cavalry come charging to the rescue before he, Buddha Chan and Freddie could regroup with Marie's men.

Something *big* was going down here.

Jack wished he knew what the heck it was.

Shoving his thoughts into his back pocket, he continued to creep down toward the FSE Goons.

NINETEEN

Crazy Jack Keenan padded toward the FSE troops. He tried to make his massive form invisible, which was no easy task. He was practically crawling on his belly when he inched his way up to the perimeter of the enemy force's camp.

"Now," he whispered to himself. "Open up now."

Suddenly, from the night sky, there came a volley of automatic and semiautomatic fire.

Jack watched the dusky earth before him erupt in a series of spiraling, whirling, twirling cyclones.

The FSE troops, settled in for the night, leapt to their feet, yelling in a foreign language. Jack didn't understand the words but he recognized the sound of panic.

Jack waited for a few seconds before bursting from his cover, his AK-47 blazing.

He ran blindly through the troops, spraying anyone and everyone who came into his path.

Bullets pinged all around him.

He continued to charge.

Two young men leapt up before him, their pistols drawn. Crazy Jack didn't think twice. He continued to rock and roll. The two soldiers watched their bellies explode and their insides become outsides, and Jack sprinted by them.

By the time they hit the ground, Jack was twenty feet behind them.

He ran for the jeep.

The men on the jeep, manning their machine gun, trained their sights on Crazy Jack.

Dead man, he thought. *I'm nothing more than dog food now.*

Then a titanic form emerged from the shadows. Crazy Jack almost stopped in his tracks.

He recognized the shadow-shape.

It was Marie Marrette. She loomed high above the two machine gunners and, raising two flabby arms, grabbed the two FSE punks' heads in her titanic palms and smashed them together.

The two gunners didn't know what hit them.

They tumbled forward from their jeep.

Crazy Jack sprang forward. "I owe you!" he yelled to Marie.

"No shit!" Marie yelled back, diving toward the other enemy troops, her M16 ready.

Jack leapt into the jeep and trained the machine gun on the nearby radioman. The FSE Goon stopped in mid-move. He saw the barrel of the gun swing his way. A strange, calm expression appeared on his face. He dived for the radio. The gun burst to life. The radio exploded. The man exploded. When Jack was done, only the lower half of the man's body remained upright.

After a small eternity the pair of legs tumbled onto the ground, raising a small cloud of blood-flecked dust.

"Jeeez," Jack said, still amazed at what bullets could do to the allegedly most advanced animal on the face of the earth. He shrugged his shoulders. What the hell. Man had created these idiotic weapons; let him suffer because of it.

Jack grunted and swirled the gun toward the remaining enemy troops. He sat in the back of the vehicle and began spraying, making sure to ignore Marie and her own unique path of destruction.

Round after round screeched through the once-silent night.

The FSE Goons twisted and turned, lurched and bucked, as the bullets slammed through their bodies.

Jack found himself grinning as he urged them into a slam-dance of death.

From the hillside above, shots continued to ring out, effectively shielding Jack from any enemy interference. He was sacred. He was holy. He was protected.

Angels watched down upon him.

The baddest angels in all of creation.

Marauding angels.

Bodies began to lurch toward him, stopped in their tracks by lethal sniper fire. Their brains exploded forward, watched by startled, blind eyes. Their inner organs burst forth out of ruptured chests and bellies, tumbling down onto their knees from large, harsh exit wounds. The men screeched like brutalized banshees as they catapulted onto the earth.

Jack glanced around him.

The night continued to disgorge enemy soldiers.

He continued to squeeze the trigger of the machine gun.

In the distance, Marie mowed down soldier after soldier, first shooting them and then stepping on them with her bulky legs, squashing them to a pulp. She charged through the carnage like a maddened rhino. Those she didn't shoot or squash, she clubbed, using her rifle like a gigantic potato masher, scrambling brains, breaking necks.

Marie took no notice of the bullets singing through the air around her. She continued to charge forward.

Mamudi and Buddha Chan continued to cut down the enemy from their vantage points.

Crazy Jack sprayed the camp relentlessly.

Still, the night continued to offer up FSE soldier after soldier.

Jack abandoned the jeep.

He ran toward the truck housing the Soviet/ChiCom RPG-2 rocket launchers, B-40s.

He snatched up one of the little devils.

A dozen men, guns blazing, ran toward him.

Crazy Jack took a deep breath.

This was going to be a tough one.

He unleashed a screaming rocket.

He aimed it low, at the men's feet.

The rocket exploded, caressed by a wall of lethal thunder.

A tidal wave of dirt and grit emerged from the dank earth.

Crazy Jack blinked, temporarily blinded by the screaming shell.

The FSE men sailed through the air, letting go of their weapons and uttering a collective, primordial yowl.

Crazy Jack swiveled around.

A bulky FSE soldier charged, carrying, amazingly, a 60-mm machine gun.

He was a big one.

Almost superhuman.

Crazy Jack clutched the rocket launcher.

Bullets sailed all around him, making the air a great deal hotter than usual.

He felt no fear.

After all, he was technically dead . . . blown out of the water by the FSE two days ago.

He aimed the rocket launcher.

The FSE titan continued to charge, bellowing as he ran forward.

Crazy Jack cut loose with a rocket.

The night sizzled around him.

The rocket caught the advancing FSE Goon mid-body.

The man yelped like a dying dog.

And then he dropped his weapon.

And then his body broke into four, spiraling crimson hunks.

Crazy Jack gaped.

The splintered man spiraled forward, his torso pitching through the air, his legs kicking up dust, attempting to move forward, although the flesh clearly signaled "no."

The bottom half of the FSE soldier twisted to a standstill not three feet from Crazy Jack's position.

Two severed arms continued to go into low orbit, somewhere above Jack's head. Sniper fire continued to blat out from the dense countryside around him.

Bodies continued to somersault through the air, startled expressions on their faces. Meet Mr. Death, bastards.

Marie was a constant, beating her way through the troops, oblivious of any threat surrounding her.

Jack heard a familiar *kathump*. Snatching as many rocket launchers as possible, he leapt out of the truck before the mortar shell could hit. Rolling for cover, he was vaguely aware of the truck, its valuable cargo disintegrating behind him.

Crazy Jack dropped the rocket launchers and picked up his .45. It was down-and-dirty time.

He spun around and spotted the lone mortar man in the underbrush. He squeezed off a round, sending the man spiralilng back into the dirt.

He ran forward, aiming the pistol at anything that moved. A wounded FSE soldier made an attempt to raise his rifle.

Crazy Jack twisted around, catching the action, and drilled a single slug into the boy's forehead.

He watched the kid's brain spiral upward and then settle onto the boy's face in a solid slice of goop.

He uttered a primitive cry as he zigzagged his way onward through the broken, busted bodies of the FSE contingent.

If he was to die here, he'd take a fuck of a lot of Russkies out with him.

He had nothing left to lose, after all. He was too smart for today's world. He was too human. He still missed his family, his wife and his kids. Perished in the nuke-out. He was alone now. He was expendable.

He snapped off round after round.

One soldier's eye flew out of his skull, flying toward the moon.

Another soldier found his nose in his hand, not realizing what the crater caused by a bullet would do to his brain. In a second he dropped to his knees. He glanced around. *Doesn't anyone see this?* No one did. The soldier stiffened, his nose dropping to the ground. In a moment he fell onto his nose.

Crazy Jack didn't care. You'll never know the pangs of hay fever, he reasoned.

He kept on charging forward.

The sniper fire still crackled.

Marie continued to manhandle the opposing force.

Crazy Jack found himself enjoying the killing game. When he ran out of ammo, he continued to run, producing a knife.

The battered, beaten FSE forces attempted to raise their weapons. Between Jack's slashing knife and Marie's sheer bulk, they didn't have a chance.

Marie squashed heads.

Jack slit throats.

Crazy Jack Keenan continued to growl as he leapt forward into the fray, occasionally taking out four men at a time in his massive grasping/slashing technique.

He bit. He slashed. He punched. He pummeled. He did anything and everything he could to kill.

After a few moments it was all over.

Jack sunk down onto the ground.

"Damn," he muttered to himself. He had lost it. He had lost it totally. He hadn't meant to kill them all. He wanted survivors. He had wanted to gather information. Something inside of him had snapped. That wasn't good. He had been reduced to an animal . . . an animal equal to the FSE jackals. He was less than a man now. The darkness he pushed back into the deep recesses of his soul had emerged. He was truly Crazy Jack now. He cursed himself—the world.

Marie staggered up to him. "It went okay, eh?"

Jack nodded. "Just okay," he muttered, wiping the tears from his eyes. He attempted to put on a brave front. "Thanks, Marie. You were right there when I needed you."

"Ah," Marie said, nodding, "that is a woman's job, eh?"

Buddha Chan and Mamudi slogged forth from the hillside.

"I'm afraid they're all dead," Mamudi stated. "We got carried away."

"I'm sorry," Buddha Chan said to Jack. "I really tried to cripple them, but when I saw how they were firing at you and Marie, I lost my head."

"It's okay," Jack said. "I fucked up too." He heaved a mighty sigh. "Well, let's try to look on the plus side, huh? We've captured a few weapons and wiped out an enemy assault. You two did just fine."

Mamudi sidled up to Marie, forming the figure ten with his fingers. "You were magnificent."

"Yeah, right." Marie snorted.

"What do we do with the bodies?" Buddha Chan asked.

"Dump them in the river and let the tide worry about them," Crazy Jack said. "I have a feeling this isn't the last we'll see of highly trained FSE personnel hereabouts."

"What do you think is going on?" Buddha Chan asked.

"From the looks of things," Jack replied, "I think France is re-arming itself. Waiting for a big war."

"England?" Mamudi asked.

"I don't know of any other target around here. Those were invasion troops. Imported. Heading for the beaches of Normandy. Draw your own conclusions."

"Holy shit," Mamudi wheezed.

"There's nothing holy about this shit," Jack stated. He turned to Marie. "Go back to your troops. Tell them to move forward and to be ready for anything. If they weren't soldiers when they started this jaunt, they're sure as hell going to be fighting men by the time they're done."

"Yes, my captain," Marie said, sending her massive form waddling back toward her countrymen.

The trio watched her disappear. "We seem to be biting off more than any of us can chew," Buddha Chan said, scratching his chrome-dome. "What's our next move?"

"We continue the mission," Crazy Jack stated.

"And if we encounter any more Eastern European troops?" Buddha Chan asked.

"We fuck them up," Mamudi rejoined.

Jack smiled and began gathering weapons from the slaughtered soldiers before him.

"Stow these, gather the dead, and get rid of them."

"Into the Seine?" Buddha Chan asked.

"Into the Seine," Jack replied.

"But they're floaters," Mamudi replied.

"So?" Jack asked.

"Suppose some FSE troops see them and report to Paris?" Mamudi said.

"No matter where they wind up, on a riverbank downstream or even in the Channel, somebody's going to know we mean business. Frankly, it doesn't matter to me. We're dead men, anyhow."

"Pleasant thought." Mamudi laughed.

"Don't worry about it," Buddha Chan said. "We've been in this situation before."

The three spent men began gathering bodies and body parts and slowly dragging them to the river's edge.

Although the battle had been over only minutes, already swarms of flies and ants were gathering on the scene. Jack began to sweat. He was getting too old for this kind of shit. Maybe Buddha Chan could handle it with his cavalier attitude. Maybe Mamudi could rationalize it with his warrior/religious beliefs.

But Crazy Jack? Jack was just a guy. An ordinary guy.

A nation had turned him into a killing machine.

And he was growing tired of it.

He was burned out, running on almost sheer anger. Still, at least he was playing an active role in reshaping the future world.

But he was growing tired of the stench of burned flesh, the acrid, sweet smell of thick, deep red blood.

Worst of all, he was growing tired of himself. Perhaps Crazy Jack wouldn't come away from this mission alive.

Perhaps he didn't care if he did or not.

Deep down in his soul, that thought frightened him.

TWENTY

As the troops carted off the bodies of the dead FSE troops, Mamudi nestled his wiry form against the opulent body of Marie Marrette.

"You again?" she said with a snort.

"But of course," Freddie said. "Look into my eyes. What do you see?"

"I see one good peeper and a glass one with a heart in it. So what?" Marie replied.

"Have you no sense of romance?" Freddie asked.

"I did . . . once. It didn't work out."

"Ah, such a tragedy," Freddie acknowledged.

"No," Marie said, smirking, "just a fact of life. He was 'disappeared' by the FSE."

"A shame."

"A reality. Now get serious, Monsieur Mamudi, or get out of my sight."

Freddie didn't move. "Mademoiselle, I must advise you. The world is bad enough. You have to embrace old customs —romance, magic, freedom. If we ignore these things, our lives mean nothing in the long run."

"So?"

"So," Freddie said enthusiastically, "life is magical, isn't it? It's a mystery. We should treasure anything that is magic, that may lead us to happiness."

Marie snorted. "That's childish."

"Of course it is." Freddie smiled. "Life has to have a bit of childhood in it or else it's totally routine, totally adult. What a horrible fate, eh?"

"You're crazy."

"Perhaps," Freddie acknowledged. "But I am proud of the fact that many of my people have been considered totally crazy. Look at the greatest mystical poet of the Persian language. Jalal ad-Din ar-Rumi. He lived from about 1207 to 1273. He was moved by mystical love. He wrote lyrical poetry that he swore was directed to his mystical beloved, Shams ad-Din of Tabriz. He said his poetry was a symbol of their union."

"So?"

"So," Mamudi rejoined, "love is everything. He has proved that."

"Love doesn't exist," Marie stated.

"Ah," Mamudi said, nodding, "that is a typical response in these times, but, Marie, try to imagine a time when love was everything. Jalal ad-Din ar-Rumi? He wrote a didactic poem, *Masnavi*. It consists of about twenty-six-hundred couplets. It's about love. It's about the heart. In Persia, mystics consider it second in importance to the world only to the Koran. It's an encyclopedia of mystical thought in which everyone can find their own religious ideas.

"Rumi inspired the organization of the famed whirling dervishes, those who sought ecstasy through elaborate dancing rituals, accompanied by wonderful music.

"Rumi's younger contemporary, Junus Emre, incorporated Turkish mystical poetry into his verses, which were transmitted by the Bektashiya order of dervishes and are still admired in modern Turkey."

Mamudi smiled. "You see? The world can be changed by true love."

Marie stared at the wiry man. "You know what?"

"What?" Mamudi asked.

"I think you're nuts," Marie concluded.

"You have no idea of the passion that burns within me. I am allowed many wives. I want you to be my first and foremost."

"Right," Marie said.

"I haven't even begun to tell you how Sunni mysticism changed the course of Muslim society."

"I haven't told you about foot disease, either," Marie said. "It comes from walking too long in places you shouldn't even attempt to walk in."

"You deny my love?" Mamudi gulped.

"You'll face my fungus?" Marie smiled.

Freddie heaved a colossal sigh. "This makes no sense to me."

Marie cackled. "Welcome to the real world, my towel-headed friend."

"There's nothing I can do to convince you of my passion?" Freddie asked.

"Nope," Marie replied.

"So I should just go to sleep?"

Marie smiled. "Go to sleep and forget anything else but the FSE. You're a good man, but your beliefs mean nothing here."

Freddie crawled off toward a sleeping bag. He sported a boner of first-class proportions. "Rats," he muttered very unreligiously. "I hate this shit."

A few yards away, Crazy Jack and Buddha Chan focused wary eyes out into the distance.

"This is totally fugazi," Jack announced.

"Tell me about it," Buddha Chan seconded.

"Why the troop buildup? If they are going to take on England, why didn't we know about it?"

"Must have been a sudden thing," Buddha Chan replied.

"Doesn't make sense. We were taken out by home boys," Jack said. "Why weren't the *real* soldiers there, on tap? There's something wild going on here."

"You know what bothers me most?" Buddha Chan said.

"Nope."

"Call me as mystical as fuggin' Freddie, but deep down I feel that Kinski's not dead."

Jack stared at the night sky. "I know what you're talking about. I feel him all around me. Maybe a little bit of Tom Bee's mysticism rubbed off on us both, huh?"

"If he's alive," Buddha Chan offered, "what do you think is being done to him?"

"I don't know," Jack said. "And I don't want to think about it."

"Me, neither," Buddha Chan acknowledged.

"The thing that really pisses me off," Jack went on, "is the fact that we know nothing about this country's political situation. We don't know how powerful the underground is and how militant the FSE is. What we need is an informant. What we need is information."

"Fat chance of that." Buddha Chan sighed.

"I don't know," Jack replied. "I have this gut feeling that we might stumble on to something that will help us out."

"Dream on." Buddha Chan snorted.

Jack leaned against a tree, cradling a rocket launcher in his hands. "Right," he muttered, letting his eyelids droop.

"See you in the morning," Chan whispered.

"Yeah." Jack nodded. "Don't let the bedbugs bite."

"It's the least of my worries." Buddha Chan smiled, drifting off to sleep.

Not twenty miles away, Kinski was preparing for a night raid on a neighborhood house of alleged Free France supporters.

He glanced at Jean Gaillac. The giant was off-center now, confused by the political intrigue Kinski had conjured up.

Kinski had to keep this geek off-guard.

That was the only way he could save innocent lives.

That was the only way he could possibly overthrow Giles Robespierre.

Kinski heaved a mighty sigh.

He was tired of being out in the field alone.

He wished his fellow Marauders were around to back him up.

A sudden thought flashed through his mind. He chuckled to himself. Damned if he didn't feel that they were.

He captured that thought . . . and treasured it.

TWENTY-ONE

Kinski returned to base camp as the morning sun broke through the heavy cloud cover.

He had let loose several Free France supporters and was waiting for a chance to slit Jean Gaillac's throat.

Jean anxiously awaited his return.

"What is it?" Kinski demanded.

"We've gotten word of a slaughter," the FSE commander announced.

"A slaughter?" Kinski echoed.

His commander nodded his head. Jean shook his shaggy locks back and forth.

"I don't understand this myself," he said, sinking down onto a rock. "I received a radio report from Robespierre. He said that a group of East European troops heading to Normandy simply disappeared. They sent out a routine patrol this morning and found what was left of the troops.

"They were bobbing up and down in the Seine like a spilled cart of bad fruit. Body parts all over the place. The fish had had a field day. Robespierre was pretty upset. He said it had been a professional job, carefully planned and carried out."

Kinski brightened, trying to hide his soaring spirit. "Hmm, that *does* sound strange. The only really professional men in your country are FSE imports. Why would they turn on each other?"

"I don't know. There's something happening here that's beyond me. Something very big."

"Any clues left at the battle site?"

"No, not really. Well, just one thing. Somebody found a

glass eye with a skull and crossbones on it. It was shattered, but it was definitely a glass eye."

Kinski lowered himself to the ground, sitting cross-legged. Not only were the other Marauders alive, but also the original mission was on.

"Let's examine the situation, Jean," he began. "We have several possibilities. I know you killed the American invaders."

"Damn straight," Jean replied.

"I believe you, although someone is trying to insinuate that you bungled the mission. That makes you the fall guy should anything go wrong."

"What can go wrong?"

"You know the rumors. Americans let loose in France?"

"I tell you, I *killed* them."

"Fine. But suppose they were just the first wave? Robespierre could have fed you bad information just to get you out of the way before the *real* strike force hit the beaches."

"That is true."

"Or," Kinski replied, "Robespierre may be playing FSE men against each other in an effort to stall his invasion of England. You know, issuing bogus orders, having his men kill each other off in games of friendly fire."

"Friendly fire?"

"You know, the same side shooting at each other by mistake."

"But why?"

"Power." Kinski shrugged. "Once a man gets a little power, he doesn't want to give it up. Let's say that the FSE successfully retakes Britain. That means there's going to be a new FSE man installed as king, right?"

"Right."

"We all know about the oil rigs in the North Sea. If the king gears those babies up, there'll be enough fuel to keep an air force or an army traveling for years. That makes the new FSE king a very big fish around here."

"And makes Robespierre a little smaller, eh?" Jean nodded, attempting to collect his thoughts. He couldn't have managed it with a butterfly net. "I suppose that is possible as well."

He got to his feet. "Well, either way, it doesn't matter."

Kinski blinked. "I don't get you."

"Whoever they are, whatever their reasons," Jean said, shrugging, "I'll kill them."

"You have to find them first."

"I already have. I sent some of the local fellows out this morning, toward the river. They found tire tracks and spent cartridges. Whoever it is, is moving up the Seine toward Paris. Robespierre wants us to take them down."

Kinski frowned.

"Don't worry." Jean smiled. "He's sending reinforcements too. We track this army down, get them firing, and then the East Germans come in and finish the job."

Kinski continued to frown.

"What is on your mind, my friend?" Jean asked.

"It smells bad," Kinski said.

"We are near a cow pasture." Jean blinked.

"No, no," Kinski continued, "the whole deal smells bad. Let's assume, for the time being, that Robespierre is working for Free France, attempting to aid the British in their anti-FSE movement."

"All right." Jean nodded.

"Then you're being set up . . . *again*."

"What? How?"

"Let's consider this maneuver from any and all possible angles, okay? We go marching off to track down this army. If they're Americans, they're well trained and better armed than we are. We'll be walking into a trap.

"And if the troops are FSE boys and we attack them, then our FSE backup brigade rides to the rescue. You're caught in a cross fire. We're wiped out, and Robespierre blames *you* for being an informant."

Jean began to seethe. "That bastard!"

"Plus, we haven't considered the fact that if Robespierre allowed you to know where this 'rebel army' is moving, he's probably already given them our position."

Kinski kept his fingers crossed. Even he was having a hard time keeping his lies straight.

"So that little traitor wants to see us dead, eh?" Jean growled. "After all I've done for him. I have been slaughtering people for six months now. Razing entire villages, just so his so-called mayor could enter a town and confiscate the farmland. I've turned young boys into slaves, women into whores. And this is the thanks I get. The world is unjust."

Kinski nodded. "You said it."

He put a massive arm around Kinski's wiry frame. "You are a guardian angel, you know that?"

"I've been called worse."

"So? What do we do?"

"Stay put," Kinski advised. "We could be heading straight for a trap. Let *me* go out, alone, and scout around. See if I can spot and ID our mysterious rebels."

"That's dangerous, my friend."

"Maybe," Kinski acknowledged, "but better to lose one man than a legion, eh?"

"This is sad but true."

Kinski raised his wrist and glanced at his battle-scarred watch. "If I'm not back in six hours," he said, "hunt the suckers down and kick their butts. In the meantime, have your squad fan out along the perimeter of camp. Get them in trees. Get them behind rocks. Tell them to be vigilant. Should you be attacked by this rebel army, the only thing that will hold them back is constant and accurate sniper fire."

"You are wise."

"Naaah," Kinski replied, "I just think too much. Bad habit I picked up from an old comrade of mine."

"Good luck, Petrovich," Jean said.

"To you as well, Jean," Kinski said, stepping into his jeep and roaring away.

Christ, Kinski thought to himself, if that guy was any slower, he'd be a still life.

Kinski aimed his jeep toward the dense forestland ahead. Somewhere ahead lay his three comrades. Now, if he could only stay alive long enough to find them.

TWENTY-TWO

Crazy Jack Keenan, Buddha Chan, and Freddie Mamudi rode with Marie to the first Free France fortress alongside the Seine. Buddha Chan drove the second truck, Mamudi riding shotgun. Crazy Jack bounced about the cab of the first truck, with Marie laboring behind the wheel.

As they guided their "hay wagons" toward the old stone farmhouse, Mamudi became aware of two dozen shadow-shapes darting behind shrubbery and small clusters of trees.

"We have company," he whispered.

"I know it," Buddha Chan replied, polishing his shooter's glasses. "Let them do the dance. They'll know who we are soon enough."

Jack rolled his eyes heavenward. "Marie? Don't these people have any *common sense*?"

"It always pays to be cautious," the mountain of a woman declared.

"Yeah," Crazy Jack said, slouching in the truck. "Right."

The caravan pulled up in front of the house and Marie ambled out of the cab of the first truck.

She marched up to the front of the farmhouse, pointedly ignoring the dozen snipers hidden in the landscape around her. She pounded on the old oak door.

"Vive la France!" she bellowed. "Down with the FSE!"

The door burst open and a man of equal stature embraced her. "Marie!" he exclaimed. "We thought you had joined the angels above!"

"I've joined the angels," she replied. "But not the ones you're thinking of, François." The two mountains of flesh

127

embraced. "I'd like you to meet some friends of mine," she said.

Buddha Chan, Mamudi, and Crazy Jack emerged from their trucks. François LaFillois rubbed his stubby fingers over his grizzled triple chin. "Strangers?"

"Americans!" Marie declared.

"The Marauders?"

"Oui." Marie nodded.

"But they are *dead*!"

"Just tired," Crazy Jack said, extending a massive hand. "I'm pleased to meet you, François."

"Equally pleased," François said, pumping Jack's hand. "Men! It is Marie. Vive la Free France!"

A dozen men who seemed to be the result of inbreeding lumbered from their hiding places.

"This is Buddha Chan and Freddie Mamudi," Crazy Jack said. "I'm Crazy Jack Keenan."

"Crazy Jacques, eh?" François said with a wink. "The name fits you."

"Sad to say, it does," Jack replied. "Look, we don't have much time. Gather your men and your weaponry and come with us. We're heading up the Seine."

"To what purpose?" François asked.

"To free Paris from the FSE." Jack smiled. "It seems like it's about time those little bastards felt someone biting at their behinds, huh?"

A massive smiled played across François's face. "I couldn't agree with you more. But what has happened in the last few days? We have lost all communications."

"The FSE got the drop on us and some of your organization. They trashed your transmitter and personally welcomed us at the beach. One of our men . . . well; he didn't . . ." Jack replied. "But as far as the FSE is concerned, we're all dead. So? What do we have to lose by visiting Paris? I hear it's nice this time of year."

"I have bad news," François said. "There are Eastern European troops present."

"We know." Marie beamed. "We slaughtered a few last night."

"Très magnifique!" François exclaimed. "We are in your

debt, my American brothers. So what is the plan?"

"We improvise," Crazy Jack said with a shrug.

"As usual." Buddha Chan snorted.

"We don't know their numbers or their purpose," Jack continued. "But they seem to be heading for the beaches of Normandy. My hunch is that Maximov is getting ready to strike the United Kingdom. All we can try to do is beat them back."

"But we don't have the men or the weaponry," François said.

"No, but we do have the element of surprise," Crazy Jack said. "Plus we have the *heart*. We're fighting for something we believe in, aren't we?"

François cackled. "You remind me of a G.I. I once met, when the old Free France was alive and well. DeGaulle would have loved you."

"His nose was too big." Jack laughed too. "Now, how long will it take you to unload your weaponry?"

"One, two hours?"

"And gather all your able-bodied men?"

"And women?" Marie added.

"The same amount of time. We'll send runners," François vowed.

"Sounds good," Crazy Jack replied.

"Any sign of enemy infiltration in the area?" Mamudi asked.

"Things seem *très bien*, perfectly normal," François replied.

"Let's hope things stay that way," Buddha Chan muttered. "François, have you seen any air travel lately? Anything you haven't noticed before?"

"Well, there have been a few helicopters, but ones I have never seen the likes of before."

"Gunships," Buddha Chan said.

"It's an invasion, all right," Crazy Jack said. "François, what type of armaments do you have?"

"A little of this. A little of that. Nothing extraordinary."

"Mortars?"

"No."

"Machine guns?"

"No."

"Heavy artillery?"

"No."

The three Marauders faced each other. "We're in deep shit," they whispered in unison.

"How are we going to take out Paris with small arms?" Buddha Chan asked.

"We're going to have to get inside the city and shake things up," Crazy Jack muttered.

"Oh, Christ," Mamudi hissed. "I mean, Muhammad."

As the three men faced each other a dozen of François's men darted down the road, guns drawn.

Jack stiffened. "What is it?"

"An interloper," François exclaimed. "Everybody, into the house! Now!"

"You men on the trucks!" Marie bellowed. "Get the blazes out of there."

The men dived from the cabs and fanned out.

"You! In the river!" Marie screamed. "Prepare to attack!"

Marie and the three Marauders trotted into François's old stone farmhouse. Jack picked up an AK-47. Mamudi the same. Buddha Chan grabbed his treasured M16.

"Okay, sucker," Chan whispered, "prepare to encounter the best goddamn sniper in the corps!"

He rubbed his head.

He pushed his gold shooter's glasses up onto the bridge of his nose, effectively hiding his almond eyes. "This is it, moron."

A jeep barreled up the narrow road leading to the farm-house.

"One man?" Mamudi gasped.

"In a jeep?" Buddha Chan muttered.

"And driving like a complete *asshole*?" Crazy Jack commented. Suddenly he let out a booming laugh.

He turned to François. "Tell your men to hold their fire."

"Hold your fire!" François yelled, totally confused.

Jack pushed his way past Marie and François and marched out onto the front porch.

The jeep came screaming to a stop, nearly running over several goats.

Jack saw the sunlight gleam off the pocket comb as the driver of the jeep adjusted his hairdo.

Peter Kinski slid out of the jeep, a lopsided grin on his handsome face.

"Hi, guys," he said.

TWENTY-THREE

"Naked?" Jack exclaimed.

"Well, I couldn't very well go waddling around in my wet suit, now could I?" Kinski explained, swilling back a glass of good, red French wine.

"Petrovich?" Buddha Chan giggled.

"I had to think fast." Kinski shrugged.

"And this fellow you've hooked up with?" Mamudi asked.

"A major moron," Kinski stated. "However, he's the most revered Goon Squad thug in France. He has *clout*."

"And he knows where we are?" Marie muttered.

"Robespierre had good intelligence," Kinski replied, "but I think I've thrown a monkey wrench into the deal. You see, Jean Gaillac is the man who was sent to *kill* us. He's one of Robespierre's biggest guns. However..."

"Silver Tongue strikes again?" Crazy Jack asked.

"With a fucking vengeance," Kinski said, beaming. "Right now Jean doesn't know if Giles is playing him for a fool or not. He doesn't know whether you're alive or not. Or if there's a bigger American force in town. *Or* if Robespierre is setting FSE troops against FSE troops to sabotage the proposed invasion of England. The boy is *all* confused."

"Dinky-dau." Buddha Chan cackled.

"You might say that," Kinski concluded.

Jack ran a callused right hand through his fiery red mane of hair. "So what do we have going for us?"

"Me." Kinski grinned.

"We know the FSE is sending troops into Paris to head for an all-out invasion of the U.K.," Jack noted. "We have no way of contacting Shatterhand to tip him off about it. So I guess it's us against them . . . again."

"*Mon dieu.*" Marie sighed.

"It's not as bad as all that." Kinski smiled. "Look. I return to Gaillac tonight and lead him in here tomorrow morning."

"And?" Jack asked.

"I take him out and we go on our merry way," Kinski concluded.

"It's not that simple," Jack pointed out. "Somebody's going to find the carnage."

"Let them," Kinski said with a shrug. "As far as Robespierre is concerned, I'm a loyal, devoted Polski. One of his boys."

"I don't see how that helps us out," Mamudi replied.

"Ah, and you're supposed to be the dreamer." Kinski smiled. "Listen, the only way we're going to get into Paris and take out the FSE is in a two-pronged strategy. We don't have the firepower to shell the city and get everybody running around like cats and dogs, right?"

"Right," Jack said.

"So we have to get inside by cunning." Kinski winked.

"Lying?" Buddha Chan sighed.

"Same thing. After the Goon Squad is taken out, who shall lead the three American thugs into the center of town as his prized, new prisoners of war but . . ."

"Petrovich Kinski?" Jack answered.

"You got it, carrot top." Kinski smiled.

"And then?" Jack asked.

"I'm a little fuzzy on that. Somehow I let you loose in the city. Fuck around with FSE's heads. Set off a few distracting missions. While the FSE is chasing their tails, Marie, François, and the other troops flank them. Get them caught up between the rotten core, *our* core, and an assault from the perimeters of the city."

"B-but," François said, stuttering, "we could destroy half of Paris that way."

Crazy Jack smiled at him. "My friend. In my country, half of the existing history was destroyed in a day. We are still struggling to regroup and rebuild. But in your country? Think of your history. Wouldn't you sacrifice only one city to save an entire nation?"

"Plus," Kinski added, "while we're diddling about the town, wouldn't it be amazing if somehow all the political prisoners were freed by some runaway prisoners? And if I should somehow find my way to a gunship? One already fueled? One the FSE was counting on? Just imagine it, François. We'll be able to smash the FSE to a pulp from both inside and outside the city. Buildings can be rebuilt. A nation? Once it falls? That's a toughie."

"You are right." François nodded.

"And," Freddie said enthusiastically, "with the FSE getting hit from the air as well as from land, it would seem logical that they'd try to get out of the city via the Seine."

"That some little SEAL has mined." Buddha Chan chuckled, really enjoying the strategy of it all.

"Plus"—Kinski laughed, guzzling a second glass of sparkling red wine—"we have a little bit of reassurance on the way . . . I hope."

Jack cocked a furry red eyebrow. "How's that?"

"Well . . ." Kinski shrugged modestly. "I figured that with communications down and all, it would be best to play it safe . . . just in case I was the only invading force in town."

"Do you always have to be enigmatic?" Mamudi groused.

"Look," Kinski expounded, "just in case I was the only survivor of our Welcome to France party at Normandy, I took the precautions of 'executing' as many Free France supporters as possible once I teamed up with Jean."

"Executing?" Marie gasped.

"In my own way." Kinski grinned. "You see, I told as many people as possible about who and what I was and what I was after. I sent them scurrying into the countryside south and southeast of here, gathering their fellow freedom fighters. If I figure correctly, every Free France suporter in the southlands will be heading for Paris as we speak, fully armed and ready for a fight."

"By Christ," Jack exclaimed. "Kinski, you are *really* something special."

"No sweat," Kinski said, producing his ever-present comb and doing up his Fabian-like hairdo in glamorous style. "I went to Catholic school. Lying is second nature."

"And Gaillac doesn't suspect a thing?" François exclaimed.

"Numb-nuts?" Kinski laughed. "That boy needs a blueprint to tie his shoes."

Jack smiled grimly. "All right, we have an agenda. It's ragtag, but it'll have to do."

"It'll do." Buddha Chan grinned. "We have Silver Tongue here to see it through."

Kinski, for the first time in a while, felt quite pleased with himself. He flashed a smug smile. He pushed himself away from the modest kitchen table. "Well, boys and girls, I gotta run."

"So soon?" François asked.

"Yup." Kinski nodded. "I have to sabotage a few roads, and then lead what's left of the Goon Squad into a massive trap. Where are you headed now?"

"Another Free France farmhouse," Jack said. "Twenty miles down the road. It'll take us two hours to get the ammo loaded. Figure another hour to get there. We can't travel too quickly because of the troops slogging downriver. They're not used to grunt work. We have a few more stops after that."

Kinski nodded. "I'll give you until dawn. Should that do it?"

"Sounds good. Just watch your ass with the Goons."

Kinski grinned like a madman. "Don't get too worried. By the time I catch up with you, there won't be a single Goon left."

Jack chuckled. "You're a wicked Polack."

"That's the only kind there is, Keenan. Haven't you tasted our cooking? Now, when you set out, you, Chan, and Mamudi had better walk point. There are FSE troops heading out here from Paris. They're expecting to hook up with Gaillac at last night's encounter site."

Jack turned to Marie. "Marie? You're going to have to supervise the loading here. We'll double back to the next farmhouse."

"Just watch yourself, Crazy Jack," she said.

"Always do," Jack replied with a shrug.

Kinski stopped at the front door, turning to Mamudi. "By the by, have you got any extra claymores?"

"You had to ask?"

"Let me have them. You can make more."

Mamudi laughed out loud.

Kinski strode out of the house.

He had a lot of miles to cover and a lot of work to do.

Mamudi placed a dozen claymores into the jeep.

"Thank you so much, *mon ami.*" Kinski bowed, jumping into the driver's seat.

Mamudi executed a wink as Kinski drove off.

On the way back to Jean's base camp, Kinski planted the claymores, carefully placing a small crescent of pebbles around each, on the side facing west. He had no intentions of accidentally going into low orbit while leading his mob of mutants forward.

He also dug a half dozen trenches, using a knife to whittle a few dozen hastily constructed punji sticks.

He carefully cut down weeds and broke off small twigs from nearby trees.

He lined the top of each ditch with a cross-hatching of both, and then, with the delicacy of a gem cutter, painstakingly placed palmfuls of earth atop them. When he was done, he admired his work. Only a trained eye could spot the irregularities in the dirt road.

Rope.

He had rope in the jeep.

Burmese tiger traps. Those would throw the stupid, asinine bastards.

He rigged his traps.

He covered them up.

Now he'd return to his base camp with a story that would scare the staunchest Boy Scout.

And then he'd lead Jean Gaillac and his minions toward the "helpless" Free France fighters.

And then he'd watch.

And then he'd laugh.

And then he'd be off for Paris.

But not before seeing Gaillac dead.

TWENTY-FOUR

Jean Gaillac watched the jeep skid into the camp. A sweating Petrovich Kinski leapt out and ran forward.

"Did you find them?" Jean asked.

"And then some," Kinski replied.

"What? *What?*"

"Americans," Kinski breathed.

"How many?"

"More than you want to imagine."

"Well armed?"

"With FSE weaponry," Kinski said.

"Robespierre?"

"Looks that way. There's no way that an invasion force of that size could have just slipped into the country. They must have had help. They're heading for Paris. My guess is they're going to take on the FSE troops."

"What do we do?"

"We either let them pass or try to take them on."

Jean simmered. "We take them on."

"If we do," Kinski said, "we should wait until morning. They're moving by night. By dawn they'll be exhausted. I'll walk point. If they've sabotaged the road, I'll be the first one to find out."

"That is a brave thing to do. This is not your cause."

"It is now. I am a soldier, first and foremost."

"What do you suggest I do with the men?"

"Under no circumstances are they to take the middle of the road. Have them stay off to the sides. Leave half your vehicles here. Have most of the men go on foot. It'll . . . be safer that way. Less noise. Less dust."

"We attack from in front of them?" Jean asked.

Shit. Kinski hadn't thought of that. "No," Kinski said. "They will be looking for FSE patrols between their position and Paris. I think it's best if we came up on them from behind. The element of surprise will be on our side. After all, since they've just passed through that territory, they'll consider it secured. Very safe."

Jean nodded, attempting to affix a wise expression on his face. He looked like he had just swallowed a tennis ball.

Kinski took that as approval. "You follow me?"

"Yes, yes." Jean nodded. "I see the intelligence behind your statements."

Kinski let out a sigh. Whew. He'd have to give his brain a rest after this blowout.

Without warning the gigantic Gaillac loomed above Kinski, his face mottled, beet red.

Kinski half expected the nitwit to take off his head, perhaps blinded by a rare and sudden spark of intellect. Had he caught on?

Gaillac lumbered toward Kinski, stopping but three inches from Kinski's sweating brow.

"You are a true friend. I owe you," Jean declared.

"And I owe you, too, Jean Gaillac." Kinski smiled, relaxing. "More than you'll ever know. I have so much to pay you back for."

Jean shook his mangy head, beaming at Kinski.

Kinski returned the smile.

Payback, he thought. You dumb shit.

TWENTY-FIVE

Lieutenant Edju Tebekka had been born and raised in the Ural Mountains. Before the war, the Urals had been a poor area. Now it was devastated. Back home there were only two jobs a youth could turn to in order to build a future: turn up the rocky earth and pray to the heavens for crops, or join the Soviet military.

Edju had opted for the latter.

Frankly he was getting fed up with it all.

Since the FSE takeover of Europe he had been stationed in five—or was it six?—countries. It was always the same: Search and destroy.

Today, riding in his jeep, he led a small convoy of three deuce-and-a-half's, transport trucks loaded with men; unfortunately many of them were locally trained.

Tebekka sighed. He was leading peasants to fight peasants. A group of FSE soldiers (probably from Mother Russia, he thought with a snort) had gotten themselves into a bad situation the night before. Probably let their guard down, he theorized.

Served them right.

There were too many elements involved in the FSE. A government had to be strong to survive. Once you mixed highly trained men with the European equivalent of sodbusters in the military, things were bound to go wrong.

The black market was flourishing again.

Chairman Maximov chose to ignore it, believing it to be a way for people to let off steam.

Tebekka saw it differently.

Capitalism was weakening the backbone of the FSE. Someday Maximov would realize this.

Tebekka ordered his driver to stop along the Seine. He was in no hurry. The Goon Squad he was supposed to meet up with probably would be able to handle themselves. Why should he put himself out? He had bigger things to look forward to.

An all-out assault on Britain.

Now *that* would prove stimulating. None of this small-time, scattershot warfare.

Tebekka wandered over to the edge of the Seine.

He stared at the water below.

It was shit brown.

He snorted to himself. So much for the beauties of nature. He turned and faced his jeep, glancing up at the hazy sky above him.

Birds chirped. Squirrels chattered. A few wildcats howled from the hills.

Whoosh!

Tebekka cocked his head. He had never encountered an animal that had made such a sound.

He felt his eyes explode inward as the jeep, not five yards away, evaporated in a violent cataclysm of heat and debris. He reached for his revolver—strapped to his side, as always.

It was then that the shrapnel hit him.

Before he knew it, he had no side.

Before he knew it, his right arm was gone. "What the deuce . . . ?" he had time to mutter before a flying fender sliced into his throat, neatly decapitating him.

His head tumbled onto the ground, mouth still open in an expression of total disbelief.

Tebekka's men made a move to dive out of their transport trucks. Bad move, that. Before their feet could make contact with solid ground, the air around them percolated with white-hot, sizzling lead.

AK-47 fire—it had its own, distinctive sound.

The slow, sure crackle of an M16.

Like lemmings scampering to catch that one last, lethal wave, the men continued to leap out of their trucks.

The men continued to have the life drained from them before they hit the ground.

They somersaulted through the air, buffeted by the angry fists of incoming lead.

Whoosh!

The driver of the first truck blinked in amazement. A meteor of some sort was heading directly at the cab. He had never seen that in all his years of farming.

The meteor smashed through the cab's windshield and continued to scream forward over the driver's head and into the cargo hold.

Where the soldiers were housed.

Where the ammunition was stored.

"Merde," the driver said as his back became his front. The ammunition ignited, sending a fifty-foot fist of fire high into the sky, clawing, grasping upwards.

The soldiers still on the truck found themselves part of a deadly pyrotechnics display as their bodies melded with the hot, dripping metal of the truck.

The men in the other two trucks were knocked off-balance. They increased their speed at scrambling toward the rear exit while the two drivers gunned the engines.

The soldiers were trapped.

And they knew it.

Several of them dived out of the truck, only to be riddled by spiraling metal pellets.

Some of their comrades preferred to remain inside the truck, uttering one last plea to the deity of their choice.

None of them mentioned Maximov.

Whooosh!

Whooooooosh!

Within an instant the north bank of the Seine was nothing more than a crater, a man-made volcano spewing out bits of metal, wood, flesh, and bone.

The various pieces of debris tumbled down unceremoniously into the shit-brown water. Splat. Splash. Sizzle.

The birds flew from the trees, their wings singed from the intense heat.

Smoke was everywhere.

From out of the mist strode Crazy Jack Keenen, Buddha Chan, and Freddie Mamudi.

Jack held his rocket launcher. Buddha Chan cradled his

M16. Freddie wiped a sliver of slime from his glass eye and slung his AK-47 over his back.

"Well," Freddie said, "looks like we managed to kick their little heinies but good."

Jack's insides churned and he nearly gagged on the stench of the burning flesh. Buddha Chan noticed his discomfort. "Not now, Freddie."

"We are true warriors," Freddie went on. "What were we up against? Fifty men? Sixty?"

Jack turned to him. "Freddie?"

"Yes, Jack?"

"He who knows God becomes silent . . . so shut the fuck up."

"I—" Freddie said.

"You're the religious one. Look it up. Hadith. It's in your big book, whatever the hell you call it." Jack stalked off into the smoke, questioning his own feelings.

That hadn't been warfare.

That had been a fish fry. Where was the dignity involved, the honor? The only thing that kept him going was the fact that thousands of innocent lives may just have been saved. Those Goons had possessed the firepower to take out half a dozen villages. He rumbled toward the Marauders' jeep, leaving a startled Freddie and a grinning Buddha Chan in his wake.

"Hadith?" Freddie muttered. "How the hell did he know about Hadith?"

Buddha Chan shrugged. "College grad."

TWENTY-SIX

Kinski humped down the narrow road winding along the Seine, with Jean Gaillac padding slowly behind him. There were but five meters separating the men. Gaillac's Goons stayed to the side of the road, mostly on foot. One flatbed truck brought up the rear.

The sun had barely risen.

"I don't like this, Petrovich," Jean said, genuinely afraid for the first time. He was out of his element. He wasn't bullying unarmed farmers; supposedly he was up against a small army of highly trained insurrectionists.

Let him sweat a little, Kinski thought to himself.

"It's very quiet," Gaillac muttered.

Not for long, asshole, Kinski thought, seeing the first one of his jerry-rigged booby traps.

A man directly to Jean's right disappeared through the road's surface with a sudden screech. The screech ended abruptly. Jean gazed down into the hole in the road. Four prongs of a pitchfork glistened in the sun, spattered with blood.

"Mon dieu!" Jean cried. "We are doomed!"

At that point the truck rumbled onto a claymore. Kinski somersaulted forward on the road, carefully finding a safe place to roll.

The truck behind him reared up like an angry behemoth, its cab rising high into the air. The cab came crashing down onto the road in flames, the men's ammunition, stored on board, igniting. The gas tank caught.

Kinski covered his head and dived off the side of the road as the sound of thunder smashed into his ears. A mighty fist of flame reached upward into the sky, charring the air around it.

Human forms, fully aflame, skittered, screeching out of the truck, trying in vain to beat the all-consuming tongues of orange and yellow from their bubbling flesh.

The Goons from the truck stumbled and tumbled over each other.

Some dropped to their knees before pitching forward in a smoldering heap.

Others rolled on the ground, leaving almost plastic puddles of skin behind them.

Gaillac's men panicked.

Numbed, Gaillac stood in the center of the road. Men were disappearing all around him. The ground was swallowing them, devouring them, chewing them up. Some evaporated in small, violent clouds of smoke and fire.

The world around Gaillac seemed to be ripping itself apart at its foundations.

Sweat poured down his face.

He had entered hell.

He turned his head this way and that. This wasn't happening! This had to be a dream—yes, that was it. All a dream. He stood transfixed in terror as bits of semisolid matter clunked down all around him. All over him.

He was covered with bloody ooze now. Ooze that had once been his devoted men.

The air gave off the stench of charred flesh and fear. He heard the surprised cries of other men as they found their feet lifted up from above them.

Through the smoke and ash Jean watched as the trees off to the side of the road seemed to take on a life of their own. They sent down serpentine tongues, vinelike tendrils, and yanked his men up by their feet. The men were sent screeching, up toward the dusky sun. The men struggled in vain as their bodies swung, upside down, pendulumlike. The more they struggled, the more they swung.

Soon the sheer momentum sent their heads smashing into the trunks of the towering trees.

Heads split open. Jaws cracked. Noses and chins were mashed to nothing more than pulp.

Gaillac stared at the bleeding forms. He had seen such forms before, as a youth working in a slaughterhouse.

Soon the men stopped struggling.

Jean rubbed his eyes in disbelief. Explosions were still going off all around him. Bodies were still fragmenting, dissolving in violent bursts. The earth was still gobbling up what few men remained.

Soon Jean's entire mob had been wiped out.

He began to tremble, still paralyzed, mesmerized by the mini-apocalypse he had witnessed.

"Petrovich?" he whined.

"Over here, Jean," Kinski called.

"Are you all right, Petrovich?"

"It's my leg," Kinski chirped through the smoke. "I think it's broken. Are you okay?"

"Yes . . . yes. This was the result of treachery, was it not?"

"Positively," Kinski replied.

He slowly got to his feet, raising his AK-47. "Jean? You and I are going to have a little talk right now."

Jean did not undertstand. "Talk? Yes, all right! But then I want blood!"

"That's just what I was thinking," Kinski said, standing. Kinski remembered what it had been like less than a week ago: struggling atop a listing boat; trying his damnedest not to be either drowned or charbroiled. The smoke on the road began to dissipate. Jean saw Kinski standing stiffly on the side of the road.

"Your leg!" Jean exclaimed. "Be careful of your leg!"

"I've been through worse, Jean," Kinski said, casually aiming his rifle at the stupefied Goon. "That's what I wanted to talk to you about. You see, there are a *lot* of things about me that you don't know."

"No!" Jean said. "Your leg! You're wounded!"

Jean tossed down his rifle and ran toward Kinski. Kinski gaped as the giant barreled down the road.

"What the hell?" he exclaimed.

Gaillac continued to rumble forward.

Kinski hadn't expected this.

He felt himself get tossed backward from the concussion of the blast that ensued.

Kinski tumbled head over heels down into a gully, his gun flying from his hands.

"Damn, forgot about that last claymore," he hissed.

He slowly got to his feet and, shaking the dizziness from his brain, grabbed his AK-47 and slowly made his way up to the roadside.

Where Jean had been a moment before, there was nothing more now than a small, blood-drenched crater.

Kinski heaved a sigh. "You dumb bastard."

He walked up to the crater, his anger welling. "You dumb, stupid son-of-a-bitch bastard! You never got it, did you! I wasn't your *friend*! You tried to kill me. I tried to kill you! We were enemies! You ignorant pig! I was going to kill you just now!"

Kinski sat down on the road. "And you, you big oaf, you do your best to keep me from hurting myself."

Kinski sat in silence for a long minute. He slapped himself on the side of the head. Damn! Why did he feel so *rotten*? Gaillac had been a killer, a butcher.

A jerk who loved his work.

He deserved to die!

Kinski had relished seeing that.

Now Jean was dead. And Kinski had caused it.

So why didn't Kinski feel better about it? Kinski slung his rifle over his shoulder and walked back toward Jean's base camp and an awaiting jeep.

Maybe Kinski was getting too old for the Game. Yeah, maybe that was it. Maybe who ruled whom didn't matter to him that much anymore. Maybe he was on the verge of becoming a citizen of the world.

A nice thought, he concluded, dismissing it.

But a dangerous one.

He slowly humped toward the campsite, reaching for his pocket comb to adjust his badly disheveled hairdo. "Shit," he hissed, sending his right hand into his back pocket.

The damn thing had busted in two.

Now *that* really made him feel bad.

TWENTY-SEVEN

Giles Robespierre sat swiveling on a red velvet office chair. Sweat glistened from his receding hairline. He cradled the phone on his shoulder and lit up a small French cigarette. "Yes, Chairman Maximov," he said, attempting to keep the quiver out of his voice.

"Everything is going well. Nearly all the troops have been assembled. Yes, our . . . police patrols are crushing out all attempts at revolt. We are well armed and confidence is soaring. We will beat the British to their knees."

Giles rolled his eyes. He wasn't so sure of that anymore. "Yes, Chairman Maximov, if I have even the *slightest* inkling of a problem, you will be the first to know. Give my best to the whore I sent you."

Robespierre placed the phone back in its receiver and devoured the cigarette in two puffs.

Something was afoot out there, he thought to himself, sliding out of his chair and looking at the green land beyond the boundaries of Paris. But what?

He had lost a crack group of soldiers two nights before. A second group had failed to report in for twenty-four hours.

He hadn't heard from Gaillac since the day before. That wasn't like Jean. He usually bragged about his deeds, if not for Robespierre's benefit then surely for the patrons of whatever bar he was holed up in.

This was not good. Not good at all.

His intercom buzzed. Giles was so addled, he nearly dived out the window from the harsh sound.

He scurried, ratlike, to his desk and picked up the phone. "Yes? Yes? What is it?"

"There's a man to see you," squawked a female voice.

"I have no time," Giles snapped.

"He says it's important. He's a foreigner," the voice replied.

Giles's eyes now resembled grapefruits. "A foreigner? What kind of foreigner?"

"Eastern Europe," the box stated.

"*Merde*," Robespierre muttered.

"What?"

"Send him in! Send him in!"

Giles trotted to his office door and flung it open. There, in the doorway, was Petrovich Kinski.

"Ah, Petrovich, my newfound friend," Giles said, beaming. "I am glad to see you. I was worried about you and Jean."

Kinski gritted his teeth. "Jean is dead."

"What!" Robespierre exclaimed. "And what of his men?"

"Mowed down, cut up, charbroiled, sliced and diced and whatever other fate you can conjure up," Kinski stated.

"But who could have done such a thing?" Robespierre gasped, really sweating it now.

"That's why I'm here," Kinski said, backing out of the door and raising his AK-47.

He herded three figures into the room. "Giles Robespierre? I would like you to meet what remains of the Marauders."

"The American pigs?"

"The same."

Giles strode up to the massive form of Crazy Jack Keenan. "I will see that you pay for your treachery."

Jack smiled down at the rodent. "Eat shit and die, frog-face."

TWENTY-EIGHT

Robespierre and Kinski sat on a couch, their feet perched upon a priceless antique table.

"You have done very well, my friend." Robespierre smiled, toasting Kinski with a sparkling goblet of wine.

"I did what any soldier would do." Kinski shrugged.

"Chairman Maximov will be pleased to hear of your bravery," Giles went on.

"Before you tell of my heroics," Kinski said with a grin, "let me finish the job."

"And how do you plan on doing that?"

"I don't want any one of those imports to interrogate my prisoners," Kinski stated.

"But . . . they were personally sent by Maximov."

"They don't know these men. They don't care about these men. They'll treat them like ordinary prisoners. I have a feeling that, should they get a bit overtired, and then overzealous, in their techniques, they could accidentally eliminate the only chance we'll ever have in knowing the strength of Free France."

Robespierre placed his goblet down on the antique table, leaving a round, wet stain. "Yes. Yes. You do have a point there."

He staggered over toward his desk, slamming his hand down on the intercom. "Monique? Tell Captain Turok to leave the prisoners in their cell. They will be interrogated personally by my new second in command, Petrovich Kinski."

He turned to Kinski, grinning. "You like the sound of that?"

"I am honored." Kinski smiled.

151

Robespierre attempted to regain his balance and walk back to the couch. He wasn't all that successful, but he did make it onto the sofa.

Kinski faked taking a deep sip of the wine. "Maybe I should interrogate them now."

"No, no, no. We have plenty of time for that," Robespierre said. "It has been so long since I have conversed with someone I consider an equal. Someone brave yet sly. Strong yet cunning."

"Well, all right," Kinski replied. "There's a lot I'd like to know about Paris."

"Paris?" Robespierre frowned. "It is a dead city. I have never liked it myself. It catered to tourists. Now? It is nothing more than a prison, one large, glittering prison."

"I don't understand," Kinski began.

"The Arsenal Library? The Chaillot Palace? The Palais Royal? They've all been stripped. They are filled with rebels."

"Heavily guarded?"

"Not necessary." Robespierre grinned. "We leave them there to rot. Oh, we feed them, certainly, but if they are to survive inside, they have to take on responsibilities. Each prison is patrolled by two dozen men with machine guns that could slice through the walls of the buildings as if they were Swiss cheese. Ha ha, I have just made a joke, have I not? The machines guns would make holes in the walls! Swiss cheese has holes. Ha ha ha."

Kinski forced a grin. "Droll. Very droll."

"We have them under control," Robespierre said. "They are men without hope. Take away a man's hope? His dreams? He no longer wants to rebel. He wants to enter sleep. The big sleep. Leave the world behind. They are a very dispirited lot."

"Many in numbers?"

"A few thousand at the very least."

"And you have no fear of rebellion?"

Giles chuckled. "No," he replied. "But the most ironic aspect of it all is that recently we have been importing arms. We store the arms on the same ground as the prisoners. Is that not a laugh?"

"You don't worry about them getting their hands on them?"

"Not at all," Robespierre said, draining his goblet. "Many of these men and women have not seen sunlight—*real* sunlight—in the last six months. They don't know what the world outside looks like anymore. They could have no possible inkling of the power that patrols the streets now."

"I'd be interested in seeing some of the prisons," Kinski said. "If you don't mind."

"A morbid sense of curiosity, eh?"

"Well, if I *am* going to be your second in command . . ."

"Ah, yes, it would be to your benefit. Then, after we have our tour of the city, we will have a feast, eh? A feast to celebrate your heroism. And after that? How would you like to spend the night interrogating those American bastards?"

Kinski nodded. "Sounds like a perfect combination of pleasure and pain."

"Two of my favorite businesses," Robespierre said. "Come, I will get a driver."

TWENTY-NINE

Buddha Chan, Mamudi, and Crazy Jack looked up as the door to their cell swung open. Kinski dismissed a local guard. "No need. I'll handle this myself."

He strode into the room and glanced at his comrades.

"Took you long enough," Mamudi groused.

"I took a tour of the city," Kinski said, bending over the men. "Do me a favor, will you? Every so often, someone yell and pound the wall."

"I'd enjoy that," Buddha Chan said, rubbing his bald head for luck.

Kinski reached into his pocket and pulled out a thin green book.

"What the hell is that?" Jack asked.

"The *Michelin Guide to Paris*," Kinski said. "Here's the deal. There are main buildings housing the prisoners. You're damn lucky Robespierre tossed you into a former jail house. The rest of these places were either museums or palaces and have been gutted. The people have been tossed into them like cattle. At least you have a normal cell."

He pointed to the precircled positions. "I toured every one of these cesspools. Man, it's drastic. Pigsty. The people look like cancer victims, and let's just say that the sanitary conditions leave something to be desired. The FSE is mainly working on their minds, making them feel less than human."

"Guarded well?" Mamudi asked as Buddha Chan howled and banged the wall.

"Hardly at all," Kinski replied. "These people are so robbed of spirit, man, they look like fucking zombies."

"Will they be able to fight?" Jack inquired as Buddha Chan howled again.

"Damn straight, once they discover that there are enough weapons to blow away half of the FSE jerks in town. The weapons are stored in the same buildings as where they've been walking in their own piss for the last half year."

Jack grinned. "I like the sound of that."

"Plus," Kinski said, "I hit a big Bingo on my tour. The choppers are stored at Orly. A dozen of them."

Buddha Chan howled again.

"Half of them are fully fueled," Kinski said, beaming. "All I have to do is get out there . . . after you've escaped."

Kinski produced three .45s. "One guard down the hall. Two in the main entranceway. They're assholes."

"Is that it?" Mamudi asked.

"Nope." Kinski shrugged. "Now you have to beat the shit out of me."

"Are you sure about that?" Jack asked.

"I have to protect my cover, right? One of you is going to have to reach Marie. The other two? You have to get these folks out of those pits. After that? I'll need someone to rendezvous with me at Orly."

"Sounds like you need a good gunner," Buddha Chan said, polishing his glasses. "Now you've got one."

Kinski grinned. He faced Jack. "Okay, prisoners, do in your interrogator."

Jack hesitated.

"Come on, Jack, take your best shot," Kinski teased.

Kinski stuck out his chin.

Jack reared back a bulky left fist.

He slammed Kinski in the stomach, effectively knocking the air out of him and sending him hurtling into the door. The door burst open and Kinski landed on his back, in the corridor outside the hall.

"I think you might have overdone it, there, Jack." Mamudi sighed, raising his .45.

"You go for Marie," Jack muttered. "Buddha Chan and I will do what we can to keep Paris popping."

"I'd be pleased to escort Marie," Mamudi said, darting out of the cell with all the enthusiasm of a child about to unwrap the best Christmas present of them all.

Jack glanced at Kinski. Peter was nearly in a coma. "Well, he told me to take my best shot," he muttered, following Mamudi and Buddha Chan down the hallway.

Before the FSE guard had a chance to raise his rifle, Mamudi had already drilled a slug through his neck. The guard's head flopped over to his left side. His body played follow the leader. Mamudi grabbed the gun.

In the booking area of the small police station, two other guards were on their way into the cell area. The Marauders were on their way out.

The guards stopped running as the air crackled around them.

The three Marauders leapt over the bodies as they headed out into the enslaved streets of Paris.

THIRTY

Giles Robespierre slithered down into his red velvet desk chair, gazing sadly upon the battered, bruised form of Petrovich Kinski.

Outside his window, the streets of Paris crackled with sporadic gunfire.

A mortar shell fell near Robespierre's suite, sending the windows rattling.

"I do not understand this," he muttered.

"They were armed when I entered the cell," Kinski muttered, still clutching his bruised midsection. "Your so-called 'guards' didn't do a very good job of patting them down."

"But how did they know where the prisoners were kept?" Robespierre moaned. "We have lost them all! By the time our reinforcements arrived, the vermin were gone. They could be anywhere in the city by now, very well armed, knowing every inch of the territory."

"That's not the worst part," Kinski said. "If Free France tipped off the Marauders as to the prisoners' whereabouts, you can be sure that they're already in town... along with the Americans."

"Maximov will not like this," Robespierre said.

"Perhaps Maximov does not have to know," Kinski said.

"But surely I must inform him of this great calamity!"

"And then what will happen?"

"He'll send in more troops. We'll beat down this rebellion!" Robespierre declared.

"I wasn't talking about that," Kinski continued. "I mean, what will happen to you?"

159

"Well, I . . . will probably lose my position," Robespierre offered.

"You'll probably lose a lot more than that."

The color drained from Giles's face. What the Polish soldier said was true. He was done for. Yet the Pole seemed hopeful. Robespierre was grasping at straws now—and he knew it.

"Do you have any suggestions?" he asked Petrovich Kinski.

Kinski smiled. "They may not be good ones," he said tentatively.

"Please, tell me," Giles implored.

"Suppose we let Free France battle it out with the FSE for a little while longer," he offered. "You send me and a dozen good men out to Orly. We take up your six fueled gunships, and while the FSE takes on Free France on the streets, we take on Free France from the skies. Those helicopters have both rockets and machine guns, correct?"

"Correct."

"Well, then, you might have to lose a few buildings while we exterminate the FSE troops from the heavens."

"Fuck the buildings," Robespierre said, seeing a light at the end of the tunnel. "Just mash those insects into the ground!"

"So," Kinski said, rising, "I take it I'm off to Orly!"

"By the time you reach the front of the hotel, your men will be waiting!"

To the south of Paris, some two thousands citizens, armed with every type of rifle and handgun imaginable, snaked their way toward the city. Some carried Molotov cocktails in the back of their paint-chipped cars. Others wielded homemade powder grenades and sticks of dynamite, commonly used to blast rocks from the landscape.

In the lead car, a straw-haired girl named Michelle smiled as she heard the sound of distant gunfire.

"Do you see?" she said, turning to the sullen man next to her. "He and his friends *are* taking on the FSE!"

"If we go such as we are," the man named Marius said,

"we may be killed. We are no match for the Eastern European soldiers."

"We have come too far to turn back now," the girl said defiantly.

A large explosion shook the center of Paris.

"You are right," Marius said, seething, "Vive la Free France!"

He honked his horn and raised a clenched fist from the driver's window.

All those in the caravan did the same.

They sped toward Paris.

Crazy Jack Keenan dizzily drove a commandeered autobus west of Paris. Inside, a lone freed prisoner sat, grim and determined. In his arms he cradled an AK-47. He glanced at the city behind him. The crackle of gunfire was everywhere. Small plumes of smoke snaked their way up over the horizon. The man was gaunt and suffering from malnutrition. Still, there was a spark in his eyes, a spark that could ignite all of France, all of Free France.

Jack yanked the wheel and slammed on the brakes, skidding into a smooth wooded area outside the city.

He quickly leapt from the vehicle, fearing a stray mortar hit at any moment.

The thin man calmly walked out of the bus directly behind Jack.

The massive form of Marie appeared from the woods, her troops now fully massed behind her. "We are ready," she announced.

The men murmured assent.

Freddie Mamudi stood in her shadow. Jack grinned. "Then I guess it's time we got going. The prisoners are freed and well armed, taking on the FSE in house-to-house combat, pushing forward block by block toward the center of town. By the way, I brought someone back who said he knew you. . . ."

The thin man emerged from behind Jack.

A wide grin played across Marie's face. She dropped her rifle and ran forward, tree-trunk arms extended. The thin man trotted toward her. They both embraced, exchanging passionate kisses. Mamudi's jaw dropped with a resounding crack.

"Jack? Freddie? Remember that farmer I told you about? The one who disappeared?"

"Uh-huh," Freddie managed.

"Well, I'd like you to meet Gérard, my husband."

Freddie's glass eye nearly went into low orbit.

THIRTY-ONE

Kinski arrived at Orly with thirteen eager FSE men at his heels. Before them loomed six Cobras, ready to rock. Each boasted two rocket pods on each side, each raring to send two 2.5-inch rockets screaming into the air. Also on board were XM-21 systems, mini-guns that could hammer out two thousand rounds per minute.

Kinski slowed his pace. He spun toward the men. "I'm afraid there's been a change of plans," he announced.

The familiar sound of AK-47 fire sliced through the air. Kinski hit the macadam as the FSE men jerked and quivered. Bullets slammed into them, pushing them away from Kinski and toward their eternal reward.

Kinski slowly got to his feet.

Buddha Chan emerged from several stacking crates behind him. "Look what I found," he said, holding up the AK-47.

"I was hoping you'd be there," Kinski said, trotting toward the lead Cobra.

"If nothing else, I'm dependable," Buddha Chan said, trotting behind him.

"Let's see what shape this baby is in," Kinski said, leaping into the cockpit and sending the rotor blades twirling to life. Buddha Chan scrambled into the ship's midsection, caressing the mini-guns. Lots of ammo. Weapons cleaned recently. "Looks fine back here," he called.

Kinski nodded. "Same here. Hey, look at this. A PA system. Damn, we used to use these all the time to rattle the enemy. Let's see what tape they have here. Apples to oranges, it's an old U.S. tune. These birds haven't been used since way before the war."

He pushed the cassette in. A well-worn copy of Creedence Clearwater Revival's "Bad Moon Rising" howled out over the bullet-riddled body of the FSE troops.

"They're playing our song." Kinski laughed, allowing the machine to lift its way into the sky.

"Let's rock and roll," Buddha Chan said with a slight grimace. He had never been crazy about heights.

"Let old Silver Tongue take you on a tour of Gay Paree, Buddha, my man."

The Cobra growled into the clouds above Orly and zipped off, toward the city under siege.

Crazy Jack and Mamudi led Marie's men down the twisting streets of Paris, heading for Découverte Palais, past the Arc de Triomphe.

The freed prisoners had pushed the startled FSE troops back toward both the Grand Palais and the Petit Palais. By the time the FSE men had realized exactly who they were up against and how many, they had fallen back.

Now they were hunkering in, occupying the hundred-year-old buildings. What once had been museums were now fire bases. The FSE sent some of their men toward the nearby Elysée Palace to make a stand as well, effectively forming a triangular defensive perimeter.

The FSE was far from being beaten yet. They had the experience and the larger armaments. They weren't worried about how they used them, either.

As Jack, Mamudi, and Marie sprinted past the Avenue Foch, buildings and pieces of street began to explode around them. "Mortars," Jack said, tumbling onto the ground.

"Eighty-one-mm?" Mamudi said as a shell shrieked into a building a block to their left.

"They can blow this whole damn town up around us," Jack hissed.

A badly fragged young man ran up the street. "Vive la Free France!" he yelled. "An army of freedom fighters has emerged from the south. They are marching toward the palace!"

The boy flashed a triumphant smile before the street erupted into a swirling cloud of concrete and dust.

"Shit," Jack muttered. "I hope those boys don't have

SAMs, or else Kinski's up the creek. Grenade launchers should keep the country folk back."

Fifteen meters away, a wall collapsed with a deafening roar.

"Marie?" he said, turning over his shoulder. "Load up all extra ammo on your last truck, will you?"

Jack skittered back half a block and retrieved a recoilless rocket launcher.

"What the hell are you going to do, Jack?"

"Somebody has to open a hole in their defenses," he said, climbing behind the wheel of the cab. "I'm going to pull a Tom Bee."

"That's crazy!" Mamudi declared.

"That's my name," Jack said, grinding gears and shifting the truck into drive. "Get ready to run, folks."

Jack picked up speed, guiding the truck through the pock-marked Champs-Elysées and hanging a screaming right onto the Avenue de Marigny toward both the Grand and Petit Palaces. Mortars sailed all around him, sending up chunks of the palace gardens. Seventy-nine-mm rounds tore into the road, sending up sprays of hard, dark macadam. He continued to barrel down the road, zigzagging as much as possible. He'd need a miracle to pull this off.

From out of nowhere, like an angry hornet, a mighty, bullet-spitting machine appeared, belching death and Creedence Clearwater Revival.

"Thank you, Kinski or God or whoever is responsible," Jack whispered.

The Cobra swooped low over Jack and sent two rockets spiraling and screaming into the Grand Palais. Half of the building went up with a roar, Buddha Chan strafing the fleeing survivors with his mini-guns. The palace's ornate glass dome was transformed into a blinding blizzard of glittering light.

Bodies tumbled all around Jack's still speeding truck as he angled himself toward the Petit Palais. By now the Goons inhabiting that structure were opening up on the Cobra, which continued to dive, dodge, and taunt the troops.

Buddha Chan continued his fire from behind Kinski. His eye opened wide in terror. On the roof of the Petit Palais was a team of FSE soldiers.

"Dive!" Buddha Chan bellowed to Kinski. "Now!"

Kinski, relying on Chan's eagle eyes, did just that, sending the Cobra swooping down toward the Palais Elysée as a 2.75-inch rocket sliced harmlessly past the growling chopper's rear blades. Buddha Chan swung his mini-gun around and pounded holes into both the roof and the men on it.

On the ground, Jack slammed his foot down on the accelerator of the truck, aiming directly at the front entrance of the Petit Palais. He dived out of the truck, rolling into a shooting position flat on his stomach.

He waited until the truck was directly at the front of the former art museum before letting loose with a rocket.

The rocket slammed into the rear of the truck, sending the entire vehicle hurtling toward the palace like a rolling vision of hell. The truck now resembled an Olympian meteor. It careened into the old structure, sending the front facade into low orbit. Men tumbled from inside the smoky building.

They turned to Jack and then promptly shot back toward the flaming wreckage.

Jack spun around to see Freddie Mamudi standing, AK-47 raised, sending sizzling lead in the direction of the scurrying men.

Marie and her freedom fighters charged forward, guns blazing, voices hoarse from cheering.

From the south came a second collective yell.

The rest of the freedom brigade blasted away at the startled FSE troops, tossing Molotov cocktails and sticks of dynamite at what was left of the ruined structures.

High above, Kinski swung the Cobra around and Buddha Chan effectively routed the FSE contingent heading for the Palais Elysée. The FSE was forced to retreat, running head-first into the still charging Free France armies.

Kinski sighed and set the chopper down in the center of the Champs-Elysées, not far from the Arc de Triomphe. He and Buddha Chan scrambled out. They were joined by Mamudi and Jack.

"Looks like we've done okay," Kinski said.

"Light casualities for Marie's people." Jack sighed. "I like that."

"We still have an old friend to look up, though," Kinski said, staring at a hotel down the road.

"Right," the three men replied, nodding in unison. They picked up their weapons and walked down the block toward the headquarters of Giles Robespierre.

The building seemed deserted.

Kinski muttered a few dark oaths as he charged up the main staircase and burst into Robespierre's office.

The windows were shattered but the rest of the room was intact.

Intact and empty.

"That little weasel!" Kinski said, genuinely angry. "Of course he'd be the first to leave the battlefield!"

"Generals always do," Buddha Chan said with a shrug.

"Listen," Jack said.

In the distance the four Marauders could hear a gentle, purring sound. "Damn," Kinski muttered, bolting from the office and out onto the street.

The four men ran toward the banks of the Seine, two blocks away.

A group of swift boats was skimming the river's surface, heading out for open sea.

"We missed him," Kinski hissed.

Mamudi chuckled. "Not for long," he said, smiling.

While the Marauders watched, the six speeding boats transformed themselves into zigzagging fireballs.

Mamudi put his arm around Kinski. "Don't you love a good fireworks display?"

Kinski relaxed. "I'll sleep better tonight knowing that little bastard bought it."

Jack nudged him. "All he bought was time," Jack said, pointing toward the sky.

In the clouds above Orly airport, a lone Cobra streaked eastward.

"Where do you think he's off to?" Buddha Chan asked.

"Probably running back to Maximov," Kinski said, "like some pathetic, whining dog."

"Well, if he's stupid enough to look Maximov up after this rout," Jack stated, "he deserves whatever Maximov gives him."

"Do you think the FSE will lay off France now?" Kinski asked.

"For a time," Jack said.

Mamudi gazed lovingly on the distant, corpulent form of Marie. "Marie and her people will clean the country out. It shouldn't take too long."

"They're going to need plenty of help to withstand the next FSE attempt," Buddha Chan concluded.

"That's what we're here for," Jack said. "Come on. Let's find a place to bunk down."

The four Marauders walked silently down the debris-strewn street, confident in their own strength and their own friendship. They were more than just a unit. They felt like family.

And God help anyone—*anyone*—who messed with a member of the family.

"Hey! Wait a minute!" Kinski said, leaving his three comrades for a minute. "God! This is my lucky day!"

"It's *our* lucky day," Jack pointed out.

"I'm luckier than you guys," Kinski said, retrieving an object from the street and holding it up. "Look at this! A *steel* comb!"

He flicked the bits of dirt off the shining object and ran it through his hair once more.

Buddha Chan, Mamudi, and Jack glanced at each other. What were they going to do with this guy?

They shrugged and continued walking.

Depend on him.

As much as he did them.

THIRTY-TWO

Maximov ran a perfectly manicured hand through his bushy beard while cradling the phone on his right shoulder.

He furrowed his thick eyebrows, angling his massive body into the small antique chair behind his desk.

It was one of those times when he wished his castle had a moat . . . and archers capable of destroying any incoming phone calls that did not bode well for his Federated States of Europe.

"You say he's *where*?" Maximov muttered. "What the devil is he doing in East Germany? . . . Trying to get here?"

Maximov drew a mental picture of sniveling Robespierre. "Tell him if he shows up here now, I will break him in two."

A hard smile formed from beneath the chairman's beard. "Ask him this question: Is Paris burning? If the answer is no, tell him I don't want to see his ugly face until both the city and the Marauders are one with the earth. I want to see nothing but ashes. *Then* I will talk to Monsieur Giles Robespierre. Until then . . . he's on his own. He'll get no help from me until he's regained what he's just lost."

Maximov uttered an evil chuckle. "And tell him to get out of East Berlin. By day's end, I will order his arrest and execution if caught in the city."

Maximov leaned back in the Lilliputian chair. He'd take back France. He'd take back England. And when he was done with that, he'd conquer all of America.

He allowed his eyelids to flutter to a close.

It was *good* to have an agenda. It was *good*.